CU00894032

Towards Th

Part One: The Fight For Freedom

Rajen and Anuj Parmar, two brothers from Loughborough, England, arrive in Goa, India, for what they believe is going to be their annual fun-packed, sun-soaked winter holiday... or so they think!

However, fate and destiny have other plans in store for them. Through ancient scriptures in "The Book Of Ted," a computer game called "The Life Force Of Xavier," super-human powers, the remains of a Saint who has been dead for over four hundred and fifty years, the miraculous juice of the Sacred Freedom Stone and guidance from a Wizard called Mikey, Rajen and Anuj are caught in a race against time to save the day and journey to the next level of the cycle... a cycle which will take them closer towards The Light Fantastic... for they have now entered level one: The Fight For Freedom!

Simon James Collier's
Towards The Light Fantastic
Part One: The Fight For Freedom

THE
OKAI COLLIER
COMPANY LIMITED
Publishing

For Rajen & Anuj... thanks

Text © Simon James Collier

Designer: Michael Sturley – sturley@dircon.co.uk
Cover illustration: © Fernando Paternesi
Edited by Maura K. Deming with Pamela Collier
First published by The Okai Collier Company © 2002

The Okai Collier Company Limited
103 Lexington Building • The Bow Quarter
Fairfield Road • Bow • London E3 2UH • England
Email: info@okaicollier.co.uk
www.okaicollier.co.uk

ISBN: 1-901155-01-3
9 8 7 6 5 4 3 2 1

Printed by Antony Rowe Limited

The Publisher would like to thank the following individuals for their help:
Christina Pomeroy • Pam & Mike Collier • Omar F. Okai • David May
Michael Sturley • Lisa Coombes • The Nagar Family • Terry Wynne

Before We Begin...

Right from the very start I need to give you some background information to speed the story along. I want to make sure you know some of the reasons of how, why and when.

I was first told about the "Sacred Freedom Stone" some four years ago. Sitting in a small cafe on Bethnal Green Road, which is in London, England, I was having a coffee and sandwich with Christina, a good chum of mine.

Now, we were sitting, happily chatting about the world and our friends, when this little old lady sat beside us. She looked first to Christina, and then to me. She grinned a toothless grin and asked if she could join us for a cup of tea.

At first I felt a little annoyed, as we wanted some privacy, for not having seen each other for some time there was a lot of catching up to do. But there was something about the glint in her eyes which made me say "yes" without giving my answer a second thought. The tea came, she placed in five lumps of sugar, which I thought was a little too much, judging by the state of her teeth. She took a couple of long and noisy slurps and then began to tell us about the Sacred Freedom Stone.

Now, I am a writer of children's books, and I love a good yarn like most people, and at first I didn't pay much attention to her story, but after the initial details, which we don't need to go into here, I was transfixed.

It all began some seven hundred years ago in India, in a place that is now called Goa. The history books are very vague until it gets to the part where the Portuguese invaded and that was four hundred and fifty years ago. Goa was then a Portuguese colony until 1961, when it gained independence and became an Indian state.

But, what history doesn't reveal, is that before the Portuguese arrived, Goa was in the clutches of an ugly and bitter group called "The Hags". The Hags disliked human kind more than just about anything else. They used humans as their slaves, treating them very badly and making them work all the hours they could.

They didn't give the humans any medicine when they were sick, didn't help mothers and their new born babies. As soon as a baby had been born it was taken away from the mother who could only visit the child once every two weeks - and only for sixteen minutes!

There was a Wizard called Mikey. He was an Englishman who had left his native Britain and travelled the world, learning about different races, cultures, food and people. He had come across Goa and saw the injustice taking place. He knew he had to do something about it!

He used all his magic powers to make a stone, a blue stone. This became known as The Sacred Freedom Stone. For every two years it would produce five drops of pure juice, which when mixed with the fresh spring water from the Dudhsagar Falls, would become a revitalising healthy tonic for humans.

This tonic would be given to people who weren't very

well, the elderly and the young and it would miraculously cure their ills. Even today spring water from countries all over the world is still very healthy and good for you.

Now, the Hags weren't very happy about Mikey the Wizard. They didn't appreciate anyone coming in and spoiling their fun. They loved being spiteful and nasty, especially to humans who they considered to be very frail and weak.

But, the Hags needed the humans you see. They needed them to work in their turquoise mines. Turquoise is a precious stone which can only be found on Earth (as far as we know). The quality of the turquoise stone in Goa is particularly excellent. The stone gave off a life force which the Hags needed in order to survive. They didn't need food or water like we do. Just a tiny piece of turquoise, which they would place in their mouth, under their tongue, which would then dissolve as the acid in their bodies was so bitter that it could dissolve just about anything.

As transportation and travel throughout the world seven hundred years ago wasn't very good and not many people visited other countries, unlike today, the Hags could keep their mining and horrible treatment of humans quiet. No one knew what they were up to.

Now, Mikey, having travelled the world and seen what naughtiness people get up to, gathered together a group of his most trusted allies and formed "The Guardians Of The Sacred Freedom Stone". Throughout not only their lifetime, but the lifetime of their children and their children's children, it would be their responsibility to safeguard the stone from its enemies, especially the Hags.

Mikey realised that the Sacred Freedom Stone could only help a small number of people at one time because it could only produce five drops of pure juice every two years. With this in mind and knowing that something a little more drastic needed to be done, Mikey knew the only way to help the people of Goa, and the rest of the world for that matter, was to get rid of the Hags once and for all.

He prepared to cast a spell which would banish the Hags to a place called "Nowhere". Now, although the place was called Nowhere, it had to be somewhere, as everywhere, even if it is called Nowhere has to be somewhere. But the exact location of Nowhere is a secret.

Anyway, to continue...

So, Mikey prepared his spell. It would take all the strength he could muster. There was a going to be a consequence for casting this spell though. This consequence was that Mikey would have used all his special Wizard skills and powers for two hundred years.

But, this was a sacrifice that Mikey was prepared to make, and so he cast his spell. There was the usual blue and red smoke, some flashing lights and a bit of a breeze, but other than that the spell seemed to go very well indeed.

And as everything settled and the sun broke through the clouds of spell dust, the humans could feel a kind of peace settling across the land. And if everyone was quiet, which some people find it very hard to be, do you know what they could hear?

Nothing!

Quiet. No mining, no crying of children - and most of all no Hags barking orders to them. Suddenly there was an almighty cheer. Mikey had made them free once again. Families joined together and hugged, fathers and sons shook hands as they were too "macho" to give each other a hug, and woman embraced their daughters like there was no tomorrow.

So, Goa was safe from the Hags. However...

There were two problems with Mikey's spell. As the spell he cast had to be translated from an old text written many years before and in a language that hardly anyone could understand, some details had been misinterpreted. As we all know, this often happens when people translate and interpret stuff written years ago, thinking that what was written really means something else. They then go about telling everyone else what they "know" it means, people believe them, and what people are being told just isn't so! Still, as they say, that's life!

Anyway, the problem was that Mikey's spell had a couple of flaws. (A flaw, for those of you who don't know, is an imperfection, something is wrong with it).

When a Wizard or Witch casts a spell, they need the power of the stars to give the spell enough energy to make it happen. When the spell is up and running, the energy needed to keep the spell alive bounces from one star to another. They act like mirrors.

When something blocks the path of the stars, even for the smallest of moments, the spell is broken. When the path is clear again the spell will kick straight back into action.

A local astrologer called Rishabh soon discovered that once every year there was a small planet which circled the Earth and blocked the path of the stars for sixty four seconds.

Rishabh told Mikey of his discovery who was not at all pleased. Mikey went back to the spell he translated from the ancient writings. And sure enough, after further and more detailed inspection, there it was, the old "planet blocking the stars problem," as clear as day!

But there was nothing they could do about it and really, in the scheme of things, it didn't really matter that much. Or so they thought...

Unbeknownst to them a little telltale was lurking in the shadows and relayed his eavesdroppings to the Hags. How this telltale ever managed to get a message to Nowhere, when no one knew where Nowhere was, even though we all know that it had to be somewhere, we'll never know. But he did. This gave the Hags a way to get back at the humans and a way of returning to Goa to continue mining the precious turquoise stone, as their supplies would eventually run out, especially when you consider how greedy they all were!

So once every year, for sixty four seconds, this little planet would block the path of the stars and the Hags used this window of opportunity to kidnap humans. They only had limited powers and so they could only kidnap the souls and ghostly images of their victims, and these could only come from Goa as they didn't have the coordinates for any other part of Earth and were far too lazy to look for any. Besides they wanted revenge on these particular people, no one else - for now! The bodies of the humans were left on Earth, but held captive in a parallel dimension which the other humans on Earth could not see.

The Hags could capture more humans if they just transported their souls rather than their bodies. In science we all know that it takes less energy to transport light particles than that of solid mass. So they could get more humans by just taking a part of them. The bodies that were left behind on Earth would be their slaves when the Hags returned. Their souls would be imprisoned in a hotel in Nowhere. It wasn't the best of hotels, there was no pool, no TV, no room service and no one dusted, but it sufficed and was better than living out on the street.

When the Hags returned to Goa, they would open up the hidden dimension and use the people trapped there as their servants.

The Hags knew they had to get Mikey. They knew that when two hundred years had passed, his wizardly ways would enable him to make more Sacred Freedom Stones, to produce more drops of juice, to heal all illnesses. If they could kidnap him, the humans would continue to increase in numbers resulting in more illness and disease which they wouldn't be able to cope with, there wouldn't be enough juice to go around to help heal people, Mikey wouldn't be able to help and then the humans would be in real trouble.

Also, if they could get hold of the Sacred Freedom Stone, they could change the juice so that it would hurt the humans, rather than help them. Disease, pain and suffering would engulf the population and there wouldn't be any resistance from humans upon the Hags' return.

Oh, and by the way, the second problem with Mikey's spell was that if the Sacred Freedom Stone should ever leave the shores of Goa and be actually held in the hands of a Hag, it would break the spell keeping the Hags away, and they'd be free to return.

But this was unlikely to happen for years as the spell Mikey had cast prevented the Hags from coming within a million miles of Earth, and there wasn't a way to travel a million miles from Earth by even the Hags' agents. They couldn't get the stone to them personally as there wasn't the technology available yet!

The telltale forgot about this little addition until a few years later and when he told the Hags they were not amused as they could have speeded up their return trip by a significant amount of time. They had their agents turn him into a banana!

The next priority for the Hags' agents was to get Mikey, and it had to be now, when the little planet was blocking the path of the stars. So they kidnapped him.

The Guardians of the Sacred Freedom Stone were put on full alert. The Hags were making plans to return. With no Mikey and only one Sacred Freedom Stone they would have to have their wits about them.

The Guardians protected the Sacred Freedom Stone very carefully, and hundreds of years passed without any trouble. But three weeks ago the sacred Freedom Stone was stolen by an agent of the Hags.

The Guardians were in a panic. They quickly referred to "The Book Of Ted". Ted was a friend of Mikey's who wrote down the emergency procedures should anything terrible happen. He was actually a caretaker of the local school, but he had such beautiful handwriting, taught to him by his Aunt Maud, that he was the obvious choice for writing everything down.

The book said: "A young boy will be your saviour. He will come to Goa on the wings of a big metal bird and be served refreshments by people in yellow. He knows not of his powers, but take the vial of sweet cinnamon juice attached to the back of this book, and make the boy swallow it. The juice will expand his wisdom and courage cells within twenty four hours. The boy would not know why he was travelling to Goa. He would just be drawn there. The Hags will undoubtedly know what is happening. During those first hours the boy must be protected at all cost. If the Hags should get hold of him then we're all in trouble."

The boy's name is "King".

There was a small footnote... "if you are reading this part of the book then the Sacred Freedom Stone must have been stolen and you have failed in your duty. So don't just sit there... find the boy and save Goa!"

The Chosen One

"The Book Of Ted" had said that the "chosen one" would be called "King" and would be travelling to Goa on the wings of a big metal bird. As the book was written many years ago and it was now 2002, a literal translation was going to be pretty difficult. So the Guardians put on their thinking caps and after many hours of frustration and no ideas, Janki, one of the youngest Guardians came up with an idea.

"Could he be coming by plane?" she asked. "After all, they are made of metal and are big!"

The Guardians, having no other leads to go on, contacted their agents around the world to see if there was anyone under the name of "King" travelling to Goa within the next couple of weeks.

Understandably there was no one travelling under that name. However, in London, England, their agent at the Indian High Commission had been looking through the visa applications (as you need a visa to travel to India) and saw one name which jumped out at her.

Further investigation revealed that the visa was for the Parmar family who were travelling from Manchester to Dabolim Airport. Their plane would be taking off from Manchester in two days. They would be in Goa for two weeks.

The agent looked through the family names. Hansraj was the father, Anita his wife, Anuj their fourteen year old son and the youngest, at eight years old, was called Rajen. Rajen in Hindi means "King!"

The agent then discovered that the cabin crew on the plane wore yellow uniforms. Being cabin crew they would be serving the passengers with meals. Following what "The Book Of Ted" had said "he would be served refreshments by people in yellow." It all seemed to fit into place, albeit a little coincidental, but then this is a fantasy adventure and you have to push the boundaries of reality a little!

Another agent at Manchester airport was contacted. She disguised herself as a member of the airport staff and arranged to hand the juice to Rajen.

Now, one couldn't simply go up to a complete stranger, hand them a vial of cinnamon juice, tell them that they are going to save Goa from an invasion from the Hags, and that in order to do all this they must drink this liquid, which in twenty four hours would expand their wisdom and courage cells and then they would be ready to lead a dedicated group of followers into battle!

It just wasn't going to wash somehow. So the juice was quickly turned into a lollipop. The agent would then hand this to Rajen, who would eat it, the juice would enter his bloodstream and then he'd be ready for action.

The flight to Goa was about eleven hours. Ted had said it would take twenty four hours for the juice to work, which meant there would still be thirteen hours left when they arrived in Goa where he would be vulnerable to attack from the agents of the Hags.

The Guardians knew that the Hags would not be able to come back to Goa unless the Sacred Freedom Stone had left its shores. If it had, the Hags would have already returned. Therefore the Hag's agents must still be hiding the stone in Goa and the Guardians must intercept it before the Hags could get their hands on it. They set their network of agents the task of locating the stone. It was of the highest priority!

Time was running out.

Although the rest of the world was blissfully ignorant of what was happening in Goa, the people of Goa knew that the Hags were greedy and after they had ravished their country, would look for other places on the planet to invade. They had no scruples or care for humanity, just their own needs and wants.

The Guardians hoped that Rajen was indeed their "chosen one".

All eyes looked to Manchester airport...

We Meet Rajen...

The airport was teeming with people racing in all directions. People shouting to each other, making sure they had passports and tickets, and enquiring whether they'd like to take a little something to eat on the plane as not everyone likes the taste of the food they give you on planes.

In the middle of all this hubbub, noise, seemingly endless confusion and brightly coloured baggage of all shapes and sizes, sat Rajen.

He was playing with his pocket computer game. It was something his Gran had bought him for his birthday earlier in the year. It only came with a couple of games and after being played time and time again, Rajen had become more than a little tired of them, knowing all the tricks and ways to get the highest score possible. So he saved his pocket money and only yesterday, had bought a new adventure game.

There was only one copy of the new game on the shop shelf. Rajen didn't know why he chose it, he just did. It was called "The Life Force of Xavier" and was described as an "almost life like adventure, with graphics so realistic that you felt as if you were really living the adventure. Scale the heights, avoid being kidnapped by the enemy, bring to life the sleeping corpse of St. Francis Xavier, stop the enemy agents contacting their rulers, recapture the precious stone and save humanity from ultimate doom!"

It sounded like a game Rajen was really going to like.

It was safe to say that he was engrossed. As it was new, there were so many possibilities and discoveries to be made. Rajen knew that it wouldn't take him long to get the hang of it, but he savoured these precious moments of the unknown trying to beat it.

"Are you ready Rajen?" a voice called from across a small mountain of baggage beside him.

"Huh?" he replied. The game had his full attention.

The first part of the game had been really easy, luring you into a false sense of security. You had to get onto a plane by dodging falling baggage. Then you had to drink this juice stuff, which sounds really easy but there was a test. One vial of juice was the one you needed to increase your "life points", whilst the other put you to sleep for eight and a half years. Then, when you arrived at the airport of your destined exotic foreign land, the enemy agents would try and kidnap you before you were saved by the goodies and told what to do next.

The plane journey part of the game was fun. There were all these rocks and things which were being hurled at the plane and you had to steer the aircraft through without it crashing! Cool!

Anita's head appeared above the luggage and cast her youngest son a disparaging look. "Are you ready?"

"For what?"

"We should be boarding soon," her voice sounded a little irritated and tired. But then when you have a husband and two boys to sort out, it's hardly surprising. She opened her mouth and was about to speak when there was an announcement.

"Will all passengers for flight AMN41A to Goa, India,

please make your way to Boarding Gate number four. This is your final call."

"That's just great!" Anita blurted in exasperation and shot a sharp look at Hansraj, her husband, who was busy playing cards with their eldest son, Anuj. "I didn't hear them call out our flight before now! Did you?"

Hansraj looked up. "What dear?" he asked in mock innocence, knowing that his wife was more than a little stressed and that he wasn't helping matters by playing rummy!

"Right," Anita chided. "Get all your things together, we have a long walk to gate four and there's simply no time to waste. Rajen, computer game down; Anuj, you get your hand luggage and start walking that way." She pointed in the direction of gate four.

"But..." Rajen began, frustrated by being interrupted in the middle of his game where he had just drank the correct vile of juice and the plane was about to land at the airport. He was about to come out of level three with all but one of his life lines intact!

"Rajen, no, just do, don't question, Mummy's going to make a scene if you don't do exactly as she says."

Rajen glanced up from the small computer screen, saw that she meant business and quickly turned off the game and did exactly as he was told. Eight years of dealing with Mum had taught him when to just do as was asked, rather than protest.

The four of them raced to Boarding gate number four. As they did so Rajen noticed some people were being driven to their planes on little buggies. Why didn't they have a buggy? All this carrying of luggage was very tiring. The people on the buggies did look old though! When he was older Rajen thought he would very much like to have a ride on one of those buggies. They didn't look very speedy, though, and the flashing light would get annoying. Maybe he could get one that was a little faster and had a stereo in it.

"Right, Gate four," Anita announced in a rather relieved tone. "Hansraj, tickets and passports." She held out her hand and Hansraj, after fishing around in his bag with a worried look on his face, handed them to her.

Anita handed the paperwork to the woman sitting on the other side of the desk. Rajen looked closely at her. She was beautiful with a smile almost as wide as her face. Rajen was certain she wasn't really *that* pleased to see them and was trying to be nice.

"Four seats, non smoking, rear entrance", the lady didn't look up as she called out. "Anita Parmar, Hansraj Parmar, Anuj Parmar and Rajen Parmar..." as she called out Rajen's name she suddenly stopped and looked directly into his brown eyes.

It was one of those moments which seemed to go on for hours, but must have only lasted a couple of seconds. Anita and Hansraj looked to the woman and then at their son, wondering what on earth was going on. The woman squinted, wiped a small bead of sweat away which had formed on her top lip as she realised she could be looking right into the eyes of the "chosen one."

Out from her top pocket she pulled a deep red lollipop and handed it to the boy.

Rajen looked at the sweet and then to his Mum. Anita, anxious to get on the plane, smiled and nodded her head. "It's alright Rajen, take the lolly."

Rajen turned from his Mum and stared the lady straight in the eye. "What flavour is it?"

"Rajen!" Anita exclaimed, a little embarrassed. "The lady

is being nice, just take the sweet, it's OK."

Rajen reluctantly took the sweet out of the woman's outstretched hand and smelt it. Cinnamon. It smelt of cinnamon.

"Thanks," he nodded to her and placed the lollipop in his trouser pocket. He was about to walk on, but stopped when the woman whispered in his ear.

"When Monty tells you to eat it - you must eat it. You will save the world!" She winked, stood up and quickly strode back towards the main airport building. Before anyone could say anything, two air stewards ushered the family down the covered walkway and onto the plane.

Even though Rajen was small, he had been on enough planes in his short life, to know that the seats on airplanes were always too close together. That is unless you travelled first class, up at the front of the plane where the seats were much bigger and more spaced out, and paid lots of money for the privilege.

This plane was no exception and it was extremely cramped. Still he couldn't complain. The tickets had been a present from his grandparents, who fully supported the idea that the family should spend as much time together as possible and see as much of the world as they could. So many different countries, races, cultures and exotic foods! It would be foolish, or unfortunate, not to sample as many of them as you could!

For some reason Rajen's grandparents didn't know why they had bought the family tickets to fly to Goa. They just went into the travel agents and booked them. It was almost as if the family was supposed to go there, they were being drawn there by some powerful, yet unknown force! This was a mystery to them because the family didn't know anyone in Goa and had never been there before.

So here they were, spending another winter holiday out of England, leaving behind friends who were rushing around, doing the "Christmas thing," making lots of food they probably wouldn't eat, buying each other presents which were probably not really needed and forgetting what the whole thing was supposed to be all about in the first place. But as Rajen was Hindu and not Christian, it was not a festival he celebrated, but fully understood and respected.

Still, the bright colours, silly twinkling lights and excitement were always fun to watch.

Rajen shifted in his seat and tried to get as comfortable as possible. Before the plane had left the ground he pulled out of his trouser pocket his computer game. As he did so the lollipop the lady in yellow had given to him fell to the floor. Rajen picked it up, twizzled it in his hand and placed it back in his trouser pocket, remembering that the lady had told him to save it until someone called Monty told him to eat it.

He didn't actually know anyone called Monty, but more importantly he wasn't hungry and this definitely wasn't the time as he had more important matters to deal with... he must return to the game and survive the kidnapping attempt at the airport. That bit wasn't going to be difficult!

Just as he was about to continue an air steward leaned over the seat and smiled. Rajen looked at him and returned a smile, though his was rather feeble as he wasn't used to all these people smiling at him. It felt most uncomfortable.

The steward had a basket filled with lollipops.

"These are for you to suck on when we take off," he began. "It helps stop your ears 'popping' as the plane gets higher. What flavour would you like?"

Anuj looked into the basket and pulled out a green one. Rajen shook his head, remembering that he already had a sweet.

"No thanks," he began. "I already have one." He turned to his game again.

"Well, just take this one, just in case," the steward continued, starting to sweat a little and becoming more than a little frustrated that the kid wouldn't take the sweet! He handed him a deep purple lollipop.

Rajen, being polite, took the sweet and placed it in his shirt pocket. "Thanks."

The air steward was really beginning to sweat now and was making Rajen feel extremely uneasy.

He turned to the steward who was still hanging around. "Bye!" Rajen called out in a cheeky manner, desperately wanting the man to go away as his aftershave was a little too strong and he felt a sneezing fit coming on.

The steward took the hint, but as he was about to walk back towards the galley at the rear of the plane, a fat man called out to him very rudely.

"Hey," he called trying to fasten the safety belt around his huge stomach. "Where's *my* lolly?"

The steward looked at him and rolled his eyes. Rajen was watching and knew exactly what was going through the steward's mind: "Like you need one!" He could tell that the steward wanted to say this to him, especially when a squashed candy bar fell out of the man's jacket pocket and onto the floor. The man was so big, and the seats so cramped, that there was no way he was going to be able to reach down and pick it up.

"Do you mind helping me?" the man snapped at the steward. Rajen thought the man was horrible. The steward couched down to pick up the squashed candy bar, not just because he wanted to help this man, but it would be really messy trying to scrape it up off the carpet if someone trod on it. As the steward bent down he dropped the basket of lollipops which fell to the floor.

The big man sighed. "Oh, you clumsy… "

The steward was getting very frustrated. Rajen could see this and went to help.

"No, please sit down Sir," the steward urged Rajen. "I'll take care of this."

"It's alright, I don't mind," Rajen assured him.

As the young boy leaned forward the lollipop the steward had given him fell out of his shirt pocket and right into the middle of the others scattered on the floor. Rajen thought that the air steward was going to pass out as he looked so flustered.

"No!" He exclaimed, almost struggling for breath. but seeing that Rajen and the man were looking at him with puzzled frowns, he quickly gathered up the lollies and replaced them in the basket.

Rajen moved back to his seat and the steward was about to walk on. The big man called out again.

"Hey!"

"What?" the steward snapped and then quickly composed himself. "Yes sir?"

"My lolly?"

"Of course," the steward handed him a lolly, smirked and then walked on.

What the steward didn't realise, as he was so flustered and just wanted to get away from this man, was that he'd handed the man the same lolly he'd first handed to Rajen.

The man unwrapped the sweet and began crunching it very loudly. He crunched it so loudly that other passengers turned their heads wondering what on earth the noise could be!

In the place we now know as Nowhere, an old Hag with

long dirty fingernails hissed as its wart covered hands caressed a crystal ball.

"So my little friend," it mumbled to itself, "You foiled my plans to give you the drugged lollipop, how unfortunate for us that you have the right one! There's still plenty of time to stop you. The Guardians think you're the one who'll save them!" It laughed out loud and then looked into the crystal ball again. "But I think not, my agents will take care of you in good time... there are more important matters that require my immediate attention... I will deal with you later!" There was one final ear piercing cackle which made the walls tremble, so much so that the plaster cracked and pieces fell to the floor.

The old Hag left, rushing to the laundry room where its best, biggest and most evil black cloak was on a heavy duty spin cycle.

As it left, one of the fish in the tank beside its table swam up close to the glass. The fish looked out and seeing that the coast was clear, quickly pulled out a radio from one of his gills and swam to the surface. Sitting on the fake bridge which had been placed in the tank as a bit of decoration he spoke into the device.

"Control," he began. "Agent Bill here. Can't speak for long. The old Hag is doing its washing and will be back after it's put its cloak in the tumble dryer! The bird has flown. The Hags know about him. Extreme caution. Protect the boy. He has the right lollipop! We are a 'go'!"

With that Bill replaced his secret radio and dived back into the depths of the tank, narrowly avoiding an electric eel with an attitude problem!

It had begun...

How The Stone Went Missing...

Under the big house, deep within the basement, trouble was brewing. For here were the headquarters of one of the known world's most secret of secret societies: "The Guardians Of The Sacred Freedom Stone."

The Freedom Stone is probably the most precious and sought after stone in the world. It is bright blue in colour and once every two years produces five drops of a purple coloured liquid which is said to be able to cure any illness encountered and endured by humankind.

The stone was kept safe and sound in a very special and secret place in the home of Sir Egbert Woodruff, the British Ambassador to Goa.

It was locked away in his drinks cabinet, hidden in an ice bucket which he bought from the souvenir shop at Balmoral Castle in Scotland. However, Pauline, the housekeeper, unwittingly found the stone one day as she was dusting. She dropped the ice bucket when she was cleaning out the cabinet and, as it fell to the floor, it shattered and ice and fragments of the bucket were strewn across the dining room floor. As she was busy cleaning up the mess there was a knock at the door.

Pauline went to answer, but when she opened the door, there was no one there. Whilst Pauline was distracted, an agent of the Hags broke from hiding.

The agent had cleverly disguised himself as an inlaid table

and, for the past four weeks, had been watching the house to determine where the stone was hidden.

The table had been delivered with a note saying that it was a gift from the Governor of Goa. The Governor, who was a friend of Sir Egbert, was on holiday with his family and could not be contacted. Although Sir Egbert was not particularly keen on inlaid tables, he was extremely grateful for the present which was very lovely.

All the agent had to do was wait. One night he overheard a telephone conversation between Sir Egbert and one of the Guardians when the stone's whereabouts were inadvertently revealed.

He now had to simply bide his time and wait for the right moment to steal the stone. That moment came when Pauline dropped the ice bucket.

The agent frantically searched through the ice cubes and fragments of bucket until he found a small glass container. It was sealed tight. But he could see the blue Sacred Freedom Stone within. He smiled, grabbed the container and jumped out of the window.

Fortunately for the agent, it was a ground floor window, so there wasn't far to fall. Unfortunately for the agent, it wasn't open! The sound of shattering glass brought Pauline back into the room. But alas, she was too late and the agent had dashed across the lawn and vanished into the shrubbery.

When Sir Egbert arrived home and Pauline had told him that there had been a break in, he informed the Guardians.

They immediately sprang into action and, as you have read in the previous pages of this, managed to locate the young boy they thought to be the saviour of Goa, possibly the world...

Back To Rajen

Luckily Rajen had beaten his brother Anuj to the window seat. At least he could look out over the clouds as they flew the seven and a half thousand kilometres to Goa.

The the plane's engines revved up at the end of the runway, and, as the Captain released the brakes, the plane went shooting upwards into the evening sky. The sunset was beautiful and looked even better once the aircraft had risen above the clouds.

Rajen reached into the seat back pocket. In it was an in-flight magazine, a blanket, pillow, some eye shades, toothpaste and a set of earphones. These were the free gifts the airline gave you.

Ignoring all the other items Rajen grabbed the earphones, unwrapped them from the clear plastic covering, placed them on his ears and plugged them into the plane's film channel. He did this straight away as he remembered how annoying his brother could be on these long flights and he thought that at least with the earphones on, he wouldn't have to listen to him.

Rajen felt a tapping on his arm. He turned to face Anuj, who was mouthing something to him. Rajen simply shrugged his shoulders and pointed to the earphones.

Anuj continued. Rajen sighed and took off the earphones.

"What do you want?"

Anuj just grinned. "Nothing."

Rajen sighed, smiled a little sarcastic smile and then replaced the earphones. He wouldn't be falling for that one again.

Deep down Rajen really liked Anuj. Unlike most big brothers he wasn't too much of a pain. He didn't bully him, too much. He was actually very kind and protective, but too macho to ever admit it.

Anuj liked music and computers. He liked mixing music, wanting to be some sort of "Garage DJ". He was one of those guys who everyone liked, but didn't really know very well. He flitted from one thing to another. He couldn't sit still for a single minute. Even if he was sitting down he would be shifting around in his seat and waving his arms around.

At school he seemed to know loads of different people, but he didn't spend much time with any of them. He seemed to spend most of his time on his own, or annoying Rajen.

Rajen's best friend was Anthony. He was a bit of a geek, but very bright and had lots of ideas and schemes. Rajen thought he was most interesting.

Another thing Rajen couldn't understand was why every item of clothing his brother bought had to have a "cool label" on it. Shirts, shorts, trousers, underwear and even shoe laces! All of them had to be "cool".

Rajen just wasn't bothered. He was more interested in his music, he loved playing the violin and writing and playing computer games. Talking of computer games, Rajen remembered that he was halfway through the game he was playing before they rushed to get on the plane.

He reached into his pocket and pulled out the pocket

computer. As he did so he felt the lollipop the lady in yellow gave him fall to the floor. He pulled it out and thought to himself. Did he want to eat the sweet, or should he wait a while? He looked at the game in front of him, then back to the sweet and then at the game again.

"Game wins!" he smiled to himself and placed the lollipop in his shirt pocket. "Save that for later."

He turned on the game and began.

Now the Guardians, knowing how pressed for time they were, and knowing that the Hags would definitely try and stop Rajen from coming to Goa, had assigned an agent to be with Rajen on the plane.

The agent's name was Monty and he was a master of disguise. He had been in training for years. Part of his training was being able to alter his shape into just about anything. He had mastered this ability down to a fine art and for this most important of missions he had transformed himself into the most perfect of disguises. Earphones. He had ensured he would be Rajen's earphones. He had been placed in the pocket in front of Rajen's seat. There he waited, and sure enough Rajen pulled them out, unwrapped them and placed them on his head.

Monty had also been trained in the ability to hypnotise people. This again had taken quite a while to master, but he was now very confident that he'd managed to get it right, as there had been a couple of mishaps which had been more than a little embarrassing. Like the time he mistakenly hypnotised a village cow called Florence to dance the dance of the seven veils and when he convinced his eighty nine year old Aunt to do the belly dance in front of the whole village last Christmas.

But these unfortunate events were now firmly behind

him and he was moving on.

Rajen carefully placed the earphones over his head, adjusting them to fit snug. The film hadn't yet started and Monty prepared himself. This was a very important mission, he could not mess up.

Monty was just getting warmed up when Anuj interrupted his flow. He almost cried out when Rajen took the earphones off, but settled down again when he quickly replaced them.

The film began and Rajen was deep in concentration. Unfortunately it was a soppy love story, the Hollywood kind where everyone is beautiful and has perfect teeth. Rajen wasn't too bothered with the movie, he just kept the earphones on so he couldn't hear Anuj complaining that he had no leg room, or he was too cold, or the seat was uncomfortable!

Monty saw this as his chance. He began to whisper softly in Rajen's ear.

"Eat the lollipop. Eat the lollipop."

Rajen stopped and tapped the earphones. He could sense a buzzing. He looked up at the screen. The two stars were flirting with each other, playing with each other's emotions. The usual kind of stuff.

Monty stopped whispering for a moment to see what would happen. Rajen tapped the earphones again, looked around him, and then after sighing returned to playing his computer game.

Monty whispered again. "Eat the lollipop."

Nothing happened.

"Eat the lollipop," he continued.

Rajen turn a sharp look at Anuj who was listening to his personal stereo, completely in a world of his own. It wasn't him.

Rajen looked back to the screen and saw that the two stars were now having an argument. They'd make up though, and then go off hand in hand at the end of the picture, that's the way it always worked.

Rajen looked down at his game again and placed his finger on the "play" button so that he could continue.

Then the voice came again. "Eat the lollipop. For goodness sake, please eat the lollipop!" Monty was getting a little desperate. Being couped up as a set of earphones was not the most comfortable of experiences and he wanted to get this part of his mission over and done with.

Rajen reached down into his shirt pocket, his fingers running over the lollipop. He pulled it out and looked at its shiny redness.

"Eat... ," Monty continued, with a degree of urgency in his voice.

Rajen unwrapped the sweet and smelt it. Smelt mighty fine. He then brought the sweet to his lips and took a lick. He winced a little. It definitely was cinnamon, and a very strong tasting cinnamon at that. He took another lick.

Monty continued to whisper in his ear. "Eat the lollipop. Eat the lollipop."

Rajen looked at the sweet for a moment and then took a bite, crunching down on the sugar candy. It tasted a bit funny, not like the sweets he'd been used to. It wasn't bad though.

He crunched away. Monty was most relieved. He thought that he was going to have to listen to the whole of this slushy movie playing through the earphones whilst he was trying to concentrate on the task at hand.

Rajen was about to take another bite when suddenly Anuj grabbed the sweet. Rajen wrestled with him.

"No," he protested. "The lady gave it to me. It's mine!

Mum, tell him!"

Anita lifted her hand up from the seat in front. She turned her hand so that her palm faced the boys. In short, this meant "talk to the hand". She wanted some peace and quiet and wasn't going to get involved.

Anuj twisted Rajen's hand and took the sweet from him. Before the younger boy could protest further or take the sweet back, Anuj had popped the remainder of the lollipop in his mouth and was busy crunching away. He smiled at Rajen, opening his mouth so his younger brother could see the sweet which was no longer his. His mouth was as red as red could be.

Rajen thumped Anuj and threw his personal stereo to the floor, which pulled the small earphones from his brother's ears.

"Ouch!" Anuj winced, rubbing his ears.

This was too much for Anita, who swiftly rose from her seat and clipped both their ears. "Just be quiet. Sit and shush..."

"But... ," Rajen began with a hurt expression on his face, as he was the one who was the victim here.

"No. No more talk. Anuj," Anita shot him one of her most stern of looks. "Keep your hands to yourself. Stop bullying your brother..."

"But..." he began, shrugging his shoulders, playing the 'innocent'. His red mouth gave him away completely.

"That sweet was for Rajen, not you." Anita hissed. "Now I will deal with the both of you when we land. But for now," she held up her hand for quiet when both boys began to protest. "Sit. Quiet. No more!"

And that was that. Both boys sat back in their seats. When Anita sat back down in her seat, Rajen gave Anuj one almighty thump and then replaced his earphones and returned to his game.

Anuj just grinned, picked up his personal stereo and headphones and returned to his world of "garage" music.

Monty was flabbergasted. Rajen had only eaten half of the juice. Now they were in big trouble.

There was nothing he could do. From his position on Rajen's head he glanced across at Anuj and frowned. He didn't look like a hero. He was too thin to be a hero. Why did he have to interfere? This wasn't good. Not good at all.

Meanwhile agents of the Hags had heard that Rajen was on his way to Goa and were preparing a reception party at the airport. They needed to stop the boy meeting with the Guardians. The confusion at the airport would provide the perfect cover for them to be able to kidnap him.

The Guardians were also making plans. They knew agents of the Hags would try and kidnap Rajen. They were busy gathering together a team to protect him once the plane landed.

The clock was ticking. The Hags were preparing for their return, the Guardians were hoping that Rajen was indeed the "chosen one". Rajen was now on level four of his computer game whilst Anuj was wishing he hadn't had the lollipop as he was getting a sugar rush and seeing pink elephants performing synchronised swimming before his very eyes!

And the big man who had eaten the dark purple lollipop had fallen asleep only seconds after he'd eaten it! How strange.

Meanwhile...

As was expected, the airport in Goa was absolute chaos. It seemed as though everyone did indeed know what they were doing, but there were just so many people doing the same job.

Anita sighed as they entered the first of many queues. This one was to have their passports stamped with an entry visa. You gave your passport to one person, who sat on the left of the desk, who opened the passport to the correct page and then passed it along to the next person in line.

They took a stern and long look at you and then stamped it. Another person then handed it back to you. You then had to go through a series of guards and officials, all who looked at the passport, just to make sure that the person before them had done their job properly. It was endless and unnecessary.

Then there was the baggage claim. This is where you waited for your luggage to come out on a conveyer belt and hope that yours has not mistakenly been sent to another country on the other side of the world!

Rajen was quickly getting very bored with all this waiting and passport stamping. He looked to one side of the airport where a set of double doors opened and out came a group of doctors pushing a stretcher. Outside there was the sound of sirens. It was an ambulance. Rajen wondered what was going on and then saw that the person lying on the trolley was the big man from the plane. He was still sleeping and it looked as though they couldn't wake him up.

From behind the trolley rushed the air steward who had given Rajen the lollipop he'd dropped into the others when he went to help him. He didn't look very happy and when he saw Rajen standing in line he gave him the harshest stare. Rajen then saw him wave his arms high in the air, as if to attract someone's attention. He felt most uncomfortable when the steward pointed in his direction. Rajen cast his eyes downward and stepped closer to his Dad.

As the four of them waited with the rest of the passengers, all hoping that their suitcase or rucksack would be the next one through the hole from where the conveyer belt began, there was shouting and confusion behind them.

As Rajen turned to see what was going on, a hand reached from out of the crowd and grabbed his shirt. Before he knew it, Rajen was being pulled away from his parents.

"Help!" He called out, falling to the ground.

Anuj quickly jumped through the crowd, pushing people out of the way. As he raced forwards he could see Rajen in front of him being dragged across the tiled floor.

Anita and Hansraj began to run after their two children, shouting at the top of their voices.

"Police!" Anita bellowed. She had a very loud and powerful voice for a petite lady. "Guards. Someone. Anyone!"

Heads turned, but in all the confusion and the sheer number of people, before anyone could do anything Rajen had been dragged past them, quickly followed by Anuj.

Anuj managed to get a look at who had grabbed his brother. It was a large Indian woman, who was carrying a plate of piping hot samosas in one hand and holding on to Rajen with the other. Why she was still holding onto the samosas is anyone's guess, maybe she was hungry!

She hurtled straight towards the airport security, who had by now raced forwards and were pointing their fingers and guns at her, and had blocked her path. There was so much noise, with people shouting out in so many different languages.

With the exit blocked, the woman turned sharply and ran towards a side door which had been left open. As she ran she turned her head to see where her pursuers were. As she did so she had the biggest shock.

Flying through the air, directly towards her, was Anuj, who had jumped on top of a pile of cases, onto the roof of a small cart from which a little man was selling cashew nuts and then leapt forwards.

Within seconds he had landed on the woman, knocking her to the floor. She released her grip on Rajen, who was by now choking for breath. The woman tried desperately to push Anuj off. As he struggled with her he could smell her breath. He winced. It smelt of musty old socks.

Just before Anita could reach Rajen, a man dressed in a white cotton Indian suit, grabbed him and began running across to the other side of the airport. As he raced forwards, he pushed Anita out of the way, sending her flying.

The man continued onwards, but was suddenly confronted by a wave of policemen. Instead of stopping he picked up speed and ran even faster towards them, shouting out as he did so.

Just before he reached them he threw Rajen, just like a

rugby ball, to another man, who raced across the airport terminal towards another exit.

To the side of the crowds was a group of what looked like school children, all singing Christmas carols and collecting money for their school. You see although this might seem a little strange, in Goa nearly half the people celebrate Christmas, whilst the other half don't. So it's not strange to see people dressed as Santa Claus and all wrapped up, even though the weather is really hot

But these weren't really children. They were the Guardians in disguise. They threw aside their costumes and sprang into action. They tackled the man running with Rajen, who, as he was about to fall, hurled the boy to another woman who was also carrying a plate of samosas.

Anuj had pushed himself off the first woman, who had now been arrested by the airport police and was being escorted to their security office.

He turned to see where his brother was and saw his little head bouncing up and down above the crowd as he was carried off by yet another woman. Not wasting another second, he raced across the airport.

There was just mayhem now. Hansraj had caught up with the woman and was about to tackle her. As he did so the woman stepped aside and Hansraj went hurtling into a pile of luggage which was about to be put on a plane bound for London. As Hansraj picked himself up off the ground he saw a bottle of cola by the cases in front of him. Grabbing it he turned and shouted to his wife Anita.

"Darling, use this!" he threw the bottle towards her. Anita, being a netball ace at school, caught the bottle with ease and jumped in front of the woman holding her son. She flipped the metal cap off with her manicured nails, placed her finger over the opened bottle, shook it and then aimed it at the woman.

"Let my son go!" The woman stopped dead in her tracks. Anita had the sort of voice you listened to. It was that stern sounding! She just stood there.

"Right then," Anita continued. "You asked for it!" And with that she she shook the bottle again and released her thumb from the opening. As it was fizzy cola, the soda exploded and sprayed outwards. The woman was completely covered, blinded for a second and tried to wipe the cola out of her eyes.

Anita stepped forwards, trying to grab Rajen before the woman could make another move. Unfortunately she wasn't quick enough and the woman regained her composure in a mini moment.

She quickly passed Rajen to another huge woman, again carrying a tray of samosas before Anita could reach him. What was it with these samosas - "National Samosa Day?"

Anita took hold of the woman, extremely angry that she had hurt her son. She grabbed the hair which hung from the end of her nose and gave it a good hard yank! The woman yelped in pain, water filling her already soda sodden eyes. Anita didn't stop there. She gave her a good strong kick in the shins, which brought her to the ground.

"You'll feel that in an hour!" she assured her and then turned to see where her boy was now.

The woman carrying Rajen was very strong. She could have been a shot putter in the Olympic Games. She put Rajen over her shoulder and then grabbed a samosa. Turning she threw the samosa at the Guardians.

As the food hit them it exploded. They were smoke bombs disguised as spicy food! Smoke filled the airport terminal as the woman threw more onto the ground. She was about to rush out of one of the fire exits when Anuj pushed a suitcase in her way, which caused her to fall. As she fell, the woman threw Rajen high into the air.

As he plummeted to the ground, the boy was caught by one of the Guardians, who had tossed aside his school uniform disguise, and then Rajen was passed down the line from one to the other. The Guardians had formed a chain right out of the airport and into the car park.

Anuj left the big woman struggling to get up. But as she did so she kept on dropping the samosas she was still carrying. As each of them fell to the floor they exploded and created even more smoke. She followed Rajen as he was passed down the line. Just as the young boy was about to be handed to the last one in line, Hansraj pushed forwards and grabbed his son. He held him so tightly in his arms that no one or no thing was going to take him away.

Anita quickly joined them both, followed by Anuj. Anita was about to explode and give someone a piece of her mind. Anger, frustration and panic, coupled with tiredness after flying for so many hours was raising her blood pressure beyond boiling point. She opened her mouth but before any sound could be made, a tall man dressed in black stood before her. He placed his finger on her lips and, after ordering the other Guardians to clean up and sort out the Parmars' luggage, ushered them out of the building and into an awaiting car.

Hansraj and Anita were about to protest, but everything happened so quickly that before they could say a word they were sitting in a big black car, with tinted windows and air conditioning.

Seconds later their luggage was loaded into the car and they zoomed off.

As Anuj looked out of the rear window he could see

airport security escorting, rather roughly, the people who had tried to take Rajen. The big woman looked at the car, and shook her fist. She didn't look at all pleased. Anuj grinned.

The man in black gave instructions to the driver and then turned to the family, handing his handkerchief to Rajen who looked completely bewildered by what had just happened.

In his top button hole was a leaf of a small green plant, it looked like a herb of some kind. Anita had noticed that the others in his group were wearing the same green leaf in their top button holes. She wondered what it was.

"My name is Faizal," the man began, his voice very deep sounding. "Everything is alright."

"You call that alright?" Anita exclaimed, pointing back to the airport, a look of disbelief filling her face.

The man held up his hand. "I fully understand," he began. "All will be explained as soon as we get to the house."

"What house?" Anita blurted. "We are booked in at the Prainha Hotel, in Dona Paula."

"Please, understand. It is best you come with us. All will be explained very soon. Please... "

There was something calming about his voice and Anita sat back. She looked at Hansraj who was holding on to Rajen and then at Anuj who was still picking out bits of the lollipop still stuck in his teeth.

A fine start to the holiday this was!

Explanations

The car sped along the dusty roads of Goa. From within the car the Parmar family could see how people's lives in this country were so different from their own. There seemed to be so many more people walking around than back home. Their clothes were long and flowing. Some of them were especially brightly coloured.

There was lots of noise. People sounded their horns at every given opportunity. Rajen thought that the drivers were being rude to one another at first, but then quickly realised that they were sounding their horns when they wanted to pass by. They were just warning the other drivers and pedestrians.

It seemed like complete chaos, but in reality it was all very civilised and worked beautifully. Everyone seemed to be getting on with each other.

It was obvious that people here didn't have as much money to spend as those back home. Some of the places where people lived were nothing more than ramshackle tents made from sheets of plastic and other material. During this time of year it probably wasn't so bad as it was warm, though not blisteringly hot. Later in the year there were heavy storms called Monsoons, when it rained and rained for weeks at a time. Sometimes when it rained too much, roads and houses were washed away.

Sometimes the power and telephone lines were blown down by the heavy winds coming in from the sea. It's not always "paradise" in paradise!

Anuj noticed that the cars were a lot smaller than in England. They were almost like motorbikes with a cabin fixed on the back. These were called rickshaws and were the local taxis.

They looked like fun, though very uncomfortable.

The car sped out from the town surrounding Dabolim Airport and then raced along what was obviously a new road as it was much smoother than the others. They passed by lots and lots of people, who all looked inquisitively at them as the car raced by.

There were lots of animals walking along the roads, especially cows. Cows are treated with respect and dignity. You see, many people who live in Goa are Hindu and the Hindu religion respects the cow.

They weaved their way through Panjim, which is the capital of Goa, then over the river and towards Fort Aguada. They passed lots of buses filled with people and tankers which were carrying gallons and gallons of water. All the big hotels and offices had big tanks which needed filling for their running water. The people did not drink this water, they drank only distilled and bottled water as this was much safer and free from bugs and other things which could give you an upset stomach.

The car slowed right down and took a sharp turn to the right. It increased speed and headed towards the coast. Rajen and Anuj could see the sea in the distance. This was the Arabian Sea and as the suns rays bounced across the surface, the water sparkled like gem stones.

As they reached the water's edge, the car turned into a driveway. There were two huge metal gates before them.

The driver sounded the horn and immediately the gates swung open and the car continued onwards.

After a few seconds an unusual house appeared before them from behind the trees. The car pulled up outside the front door and two men suddenly appeared, opened the car door and the Parmar family, after being greeted with beaming smiles, were escorted into the house.

Inside the rooms were sparsely furnished. The floors were marble and there were a few lush green plants placed against the reddish looking pillars. The ceiling had lots of panels. Inside each of the panels was a detailed scene. It was so high up that Rajen could not make out what the scenes were depicting. Each of the panels was surrounded by gold plaster. Rajen later discovered that it was real gold and that there were real diamonds and other precious jewels and gems encrusted within the pictures.

They were ushered into a large room which opened out onto a terrace overlooking the Arabian Sea. They were asked to sit at a table and served freshly squeezed mango juice. There were five seats at the table.

Even though their treatment was fabulous, Anita was feeling extremely uncomfortable. What did these people want? Why was there all that commotion at the airport? Why wasn't anyone answering their questions, that's when they were allowed to ask a question in the first place!

Onto the terraced stepped the man in black, who had introduced himself as Faizal.

"Anita, Hansraj, Anuj and little Rajen," he began. His face held a smile which was both warm and comforting. Anita began to push herself up from the seat and open her mouth, when Faizal moved across to where she was sitting and very gently placed his hand on her shoulder. "I know you must have a hundred and one questions. If you'll allow me, I will explain all."

Faizal looked at each of them. Anita sighed loudly and squinted. "I really hope there's a good explanation for all of this. If not then I want to speak to the Holiday Representative and find out what on earth is going on. We're just here on holiday. What's with the cloak and dagger stuff?"

Faizal poured himself a glass of juice and sat at the empty fifth seat.

"There isn't much time and I need to fill you in as quickly as possible," he stopped as two waiters brought a mountain of beautiful looking, and smelling, food to the table. After they had placed the dishes on the table they left and Faizal continued. "Please, help yourself," he waved his hand across the food before them.

Anita and Hansraj didn't feel particularly hungry at that point, but the boys dived in and began devouring the delicious dishes.

"If you will let me explain, from the beginning," Faizal began, "this will all become clear. How ever fantastic and unbelievable you might think it all is, it's all true and we *do* need your help!"

Anita folded her arms, her body language telling their host that "this had better be good!"

Faizal began. He explained what you already know, about the Hags, the ghosts and trapped souls in the Hotel. He told them about Mikey the Wizard, the Sacred Freedom Stone, the five drops of juice it produced every two years and that mixing this with water from the Dudhsagar Falls helped cure the ills of so many people. He went on to the Hags agents, about how they were the ones who tried to kidnap Rajen at the airport and finally

45

about the translation from "The Book Of Ted."

Anita raised her eyebrows, which the rest of her family knew meant that this whole story wasn't washing with her in the slightest.

Faizal continued, sensing this: "The Hags' agents have stolen the stone from its hiding place. The stone is still within Goa as the Hags have not yet returned, and cannot whilst it is still on our shores."

"And where do we come in to all of this?" Anita began. "Saying, just for a moment, that I believe even the smallest part of this story."

"Rajen is the 'chosen one'!" he replied with absolute conviction.

Anita looked across the table at her youngest who was busily eating. His face was covered with a sugary powder from the dessert he was chomping.

She turned to face Faizal again. "Are you absolutely sure about that fact?"

There was slight hesitation in Faizal's voice. "Well..., we did think..., well..., that... There is a problem which we didn't anticipate."

"And that is?" Anita asked.

"That your other son..."

"Anuj!"

"Yes, Anuj. Well he ate half of the juice which we had turned into a lollipop and we aren't sure that the small amount of juice that Rajen actually ate will be enough to expand his courage and wisdom cells! To be honest!"

"You really believe that that juice is needed to expand his courage and wisdom cells?" Her tone was most indignant.

Faizal held up his hands in defence. "I apologise. I didn't want to insult you or your children. I am sure they are of the highest intelligence and..."

He broke off in mid-sentence as they both watched Rajen throwing small cashew nuts across the table at Anuj, who was catching them in his mouth.

Anita sighed, placed her hands on the arms of the chair and was about to get up. "Mr Faizal. I am sure you all absolutely and fully believe this story. I am more than a little concerned that, for apparently no reason whatsoever, other than the fact we have come to Goa, on a plane and my son's name translates as 'King' and that there was some sort of disturbance at the airport which I am sure can be easily explained, you really don't have much to go on!" Anita stood and walked to the edge of the terrace and waved her arms out towards the ocean.

"What a beautiful view," she sighed and then under her breath, more to herself than for anyone else to hear. "All is well with the world."

"Do you really think so?"

Anita broke from her trance-like state and turned sharply, and faced Faizal.

"Sorry, I didn't mean to startle you," he apologised. "If you do not believe me then there's nothing I can do about that." He shrugged. "But let me ask you this. Is it all simply coincidence, all that has happened? Your parents buying tickets for Goa, the trouble at the airport and the writings of Ted! Or is there, could there, be something more?"

Anita wasn't convinced. She was a community worker back home and had heard more stories, excuses and broken promises than she cared to remember.

"I still don't believe you Faizal, sorry!"

Faizal shrugged his shoulders and smiled. "Then please allow me to extend my hospitality. Would you and your family like to stay here at this house and use all it's excellent facilities, like a pool, sauna, jacuzzi, satellite TV..."

As soon as Anuj heard "satellite TV" his ears pricked up, as he knew full well that the hotel where they were supposed to be staying that night didn't have any television sets, let alone satellite TV.

"Please Mum, can we stay, just for one night, please?" It was that whining begging sound which Anita just couldn't stand, that made her quickly nod her head, much to the delight of Rajen and Anuj, and Faizal.

For at least Faizal could still keep his eye on Rajen as there was still a few hours to go before the juice was supposed to start working.

"But!" Anita called out which made everyone hush instantly. "Only until the morning, when I insist you take us to Dona Paula, and to the hotel where we are supposed to be staying. I also want you to call the hotel manager and let him know that we will be there tomorrow - without fail!"

Faizal nodded and called over to one of the men dressed all in white. He whispered in his ear and the man immediately left. Faizal had asked him to go and prepare the guest rooms, not call the hotel where the Parmar family were supposed to be staying. He didn't want the Hags' agents to know the exact location of Rajen.

"Mohammad will show you to your rooms," Faizal waved for his colleague to come forwards. "If there is anything you need then please just ask."

Anita, Hansraj, Anuj and Rajen were all shown to their rooms. Anita insisted that the boys shared a room, she still felt a little uneasy about being in this place, though the luxurious facilities were more than appealing and a good bubble in a jacuzzi was exactly what she could do with right now.

The boys went off to play in the pool and then to the TV room where they watched just about every channel they could in the shortest possible amount of time. Hansraj ventured into the library, which was very extensive. Being a librarian, he was always interested in local history and people. With the books available to him here, he would be able to find out so much information. It was too good to be true.

In the library he was met by an elderly man called Joseph who was in charge and ensured that the records were kept in perfect order.

"Do you mind if I have a look around?" Hansraj asked.

"Of course not," Joseph was more than pleased to have company as he was on his own most of the time and had no one to talk to. The other Guardians were people of action, not scholarly book lovers. "Please sit," he pointed to the table. "I will show you our very special and prized book, 'The Book Of Ted.'"

Hansraj could see that Joseph was extremely proud of this book and was delighted to be able to show the contents to another scholar.

"I would be most honoured," Hansraj replied. "I have heard much about this book and would very much like to see it for myself."

Joseph brought the book over and, pouring a cup of tea, began to explain the history of the book and what it meant to the Guardians, and, more importantly, the future of their beloved Goa.

Hansraj felt a strange feeling coming over him as he turned the pages of the book. A warm tingling sensation and the feeling that somehow, at some time, he had been in this place before.

The Plan Revealed

The Hags weren't at all happy with their agents in Goa. They hadn't managed to prevent the Guardians making contact with Rajen, despite many attempts to stop them.

At least the agents still had the Sacred Freedom Stone, and as soon as it had been taken to the designated place and the instructions followed to the letter, the gate would be smashed and Mikey's spell broken, allowing the Hags to return to Earth.

The stone was at that moment being transported from a beach shack on Majorda Beach to the Mamai Devi Temple in the southern part of Goa. The following evening the stone would be taken to a small temple in Ponda. It was so small that only a few people knew it actually existed.

Years before, when the Portuguese ruled Goa, they destroyed most of the Hindu temples and built big churches, as they wanted people to be of the Catholic faith. Whilst many converted, some didn't want to and continued to visit their temples which were well hidden from prying eyes.

The temple at Ponda had a special rock hidden behind some shrubbery in the grounds. The Hags had discovered that it was made of an ore which would react with the Sacred Freedom Stone when they touched each other.

When they came into contact, a phenomenal burst of energy would be created. If they timed it just right, the force of energy would be strong enough to counteract Mikey's spell. It was tricky, but if the timing was precise, they could do it.

You see they had spent years and years trying to figure out a way to get around Mikey's spell. They had imprisoned a number of the greatest astrologers and scientists living in Goa and forced them to figure out a way to get them back. At first the scientists and astrologers wouldn't help, but when the Hags told them that they'd take their families when the star's path was next broken, they gave in and worked to find the answer.

It took years, but eventually a theory was formulated and after further investigation it was agreed by all that this was indeed a way to get around Mikey's spell.

The Sacred Freedom Stone needed to be placed on this special rock. When placed there, the stone would be at the right height and angle for the power it created to be able to bounce a beam of light to a passing star, which would then reflect light at its nearest star, which in turn would reflect it to the next. And then the next to the next and so on. As it did so, the beam would become much more powerful.

Enough power would be created by all the stars joining together and the last star in line would then be placed in such a way that it would return the beam of light to it's source and smash it into a million pieces. And the source was the Sacred Freedom Stone. The Hags' agents didn't need to take the stone away. They simply needed to destroy it!

The Guardians had agents all over Goa, all looking for the stone, and so far no one had come up with even the smallest of clues as to its whereabouts.

What was confusing the Guardians was the fact that although the Hags had found a way to contact their agents, which must have been within the sixty four second window of opportunity each year, how were they going to pass the Sacred Freedom Stone to them?

Even though the agents had stolen the stone, they could not pass it to a Hag as no one knew exactly where Nowhere was, and the Hags couldn't come and take it from Earth because of the million mile exclusion zone Mikey created in his spell.

No, they had other plans. The Hags had thought of another way to get back to Earth. They did indeed have the stone and needed its powers to help aid their plan, but there was something afoot which the Guardians had not thought of or even expected.

As the stone was moved from its location on Majorda Beach, Hansraj was busy reading through volume upon volume of local history, facts and dates which went back for hundreds and hundreds of years.

He had read the translations which Mikey had used to cast his spell and then cast his eyes over the infamous "Book Of Ted." There were some points which didn't make sense to him and, after scrabbling around and finding some paper and a pencil, began making notes and comments.

Anuj and Rajen had had their fill of satellite TV and had decided to jump back into the pool. Rajen was beginning to feel a little strange. It was almost as if his whole body was tingling. As they were playing in the pool, he looked across at Anuj who was being annoying as usual and stealing the ball. He hogged it the whole time and never passed it to him.

Rajen suddenly gave a long hard stare at Anuj and squinted his eyes. The water around Anuj started to bubble. It began spraying upwards and then in an instant Anuj lifted right out of the water and was floating in their air.

"Aaaahhhh!!!!" he cried out, waving his arms around, shouting at his younger brother. "What are you doing?"

"Wishing you would stop hogging the ball and play properly!" Rajen replied and then shook his head and snapped out of his stare.

There was an almighty splash as Anuj fell back into the pool. When he surfaced he wiped the water from his eyes and started at Rajen. "How did you do that?"

Rajen simply shrugged. "Don't know! Just wished it I guess!"

From the rear of the pool house the doors opened and in rushed Anita. Her face was in a mud pack and head wrapped in a warm towel. Although she wanted to shout at the boys, she couldn't as the mud was so tight it prevented her mouth from being able to move very much.

"What is going on here?" she called out as loud as she could.

Rajen was about to reply when in from behind Anita strode Hansraj, Faizal and two others.

"Boys," Hansraj asked, taking off his glasses, which meant that he wasn't amused at their behaviour. When their Dad took off his glasses as he was speaking to them, both Anuj and Rajen knew they were in big trouble. "What is going on here? I am in the middle of some important discoveries and you are making so much noise that I'm finding it very hard to think straight!"

"It's Rajen," Anuj protested, pointed at his younger brother. "He... "

Anuj stopped for he could see that expressions on his

parents' faces were telling him that they weren't going to believe a single word. He simply shrugged slapped the water with his hand. "We were messing around and it got kinda loud. That's all!"

Rajen looked at Anuj with his eyes wide open. "What?" He exclaimed in disbelief, turning to face the group standing staring at them. "No we weren't. I looked at Anuj and got annoyed 'cause he wouldn't give me the ball and wished that he'd just get out of the water and leave me alone. Then the water started bubbling and splashing and he went high out of the water and stayed there until I had a different thought!" Rajen gulped.

Faizal clapped his hands and turned to Anita. "Do you believe now?"

Anita sighed. "It's just some story my son is telling you. He does this all the time, an over active imagination. He's a fantastic kid and I love him, but believe me, when you deal with it twenty four seven, you can see the signs!" She turned back to Rajen. "OK! Do it again!"

"What! Now?"

"If you're telling me the truth then you can do it again and make Anuj lift out of the water!"

"But!" Rajen protested.

"Yeah," Anuj beamed. "Let's do it again!"

"Please," Faizal encouraged. "Show us your powers."

"Please don't encourage him with this 'power' thing," Hansraj pleaded. "You're not the ones who are going to have to live with it."

All eyes turned back to Rajen who rolled his eyes back and turned to face Anuj again, who was bracing himself to be lifted out of the water.

Rajen thought about lifting Anuj. Nothing happened. He thought harder. Still nothing happened. Anita folded her arms. Rajen knew he was going to be in big trouble if nothing happened.

He faced Anuj again and thought the biggest thought he could and then it happened again. The bubbling started, the water splashed and Anuj rose up high out of the water.

Anuj stretched his arms out as if he could fly. Rajen thought this was very funny and then started to make him fly all over the room, swooping down on the group of astonished and bewildered adults who now just stood there with their mouths open. Anuj laughed and laughed. Rajen thought this was most fun and made his brother swoop down on his Mum and Dad again.

As Anuj swooped down he reached out his hand and pulled the towel from his mother's head. He knew she'd tell him off later, but it just didn't matter as it was worth it.

Hansraj could see that his wife was starting to wobble and quickly reached for one of the pool side chairs and sat her down.

Rajen started to get tired and brought Anuj over the pool again where he landed him in the biggest belly flop either of them had ever seen.

When Anuj had landed he joined Rajen and gave him a "high five." They both then turned to face the adults who were still looking at them in shock.

It was Hansraj who was now feeling a little light-headed and started to fall. Anuj saw and in an instant he rushed forwards.

He moved so quickly that he was actually walking on the water's surface. Within a second he had crossed the pool, grabbed a chair and placed it behind his father as Hansraj collapsed into it. Anuj moved so quickly that there was a rush of air still blowing through the pool house.

There was silence. It was one of those moments when no one could possibly say anything. Anuj was getting cold standing on the side of the pool and jumped back in to join his brother.

After a few moments, Faizal stepped forwards and crouched at the side of the pool. He cocked his head to one side and looked at the two boys. As each had eaten half of the lollipop they both must have some of the power of the juice Ted had told them about.

Faizal jumped down into the pool, still fully clothed and waded out to where the boys were standing.

"How did you do that? What you just did?" He frowned. "Is it your powers? Do you feel you have special powers?"

Anuj and Rajen looked to each other and shrugged.

"Don't know!" Rajen blurted

Faizal was lost for words. "The Book Of Ted" had been right, only the power of the juice was now in both boys, not just Rajen. Before he could think another thought, Janki, the youngest of the Guardians burst into the room. All eyes turned to her.

"We have a problem," she began, her voice rushed and a little breathless. "Guardian Joseph has discovered what might be happening with the Sacred Freedom Stone and why the agents took it!"

"We know why the agents took it," Faizal pointed out. "To break Mikey's spell and allow the Hags back to Goa!"

"But how were they going to get it to them," Janki pointed out. "They can't come within a million miles of Earth and their agents don't have the means or ways to get it to them!"

"Your point?" Faizal asked.

"I think you should all come to the library and speak with Joseph... and quickly!"

They all raced to the library where Joseph was waiting for them, a more than worried look filling his face.

A Worrying Development

As they entered the library, Joseph was crouched over a pile of manuscripts. They could tell it was serious as the librarian didn't even look up and tell them to keep the noise down. Something he usually did as he thought people were often far too noisy in his library.

They gathered around the table where he was working and waited. Joseph didn't raise his head for a while, just waved for Hansraj to come and join him. Together they looked over some ancient writings and then cross referenced to a much smaller book. Joseph sighed and looked up, taking off his glasses and wiping his brow.

"There is a problem," he began. "One that none of us thought about. You see, the Hags don't need to actually hold the Sacred Freedom Stone in the palm of their hands, as we all thought!" He placed his hand on Hansraj's shoulder and patted. "This guy discovered something none of us had seen."

"Which is?" Janki urged for him to continue.

Hansraj broke in. "In this section of text it clearly states what you have all been led to believe. You all thought that the agents had stolen the stone in order to hand it back to the Hags. But as we all know, there was no way they were going to be able to get the stone to them. In the writings..." he shuffled the papers around on the desk and pointed to the page with the strange looking text. "The general interpretation was that the Hags needed to have the stone. What the text really says is that the Hags could not return if the stone was still within Goa's borders."

"Can someone please get to the point!" Faizal was beginning to get very impatient, sensing that time was fast running out and they had to leap into action instantly. "And how come Hansraj, having never even seen this ancient text can understand what it's saying?"

Both Hansraj and Joseph simply shrugged their shoulders as neither had an answer.

"They are going to destroy the stone!" Joseph continued in a quiet yet assured tone.

"What!" Faizal exclaimed.

"The agents are going to destroy the stone. There is a small addition here," he pointed some very faint words written down the side of the main text. "When the stone has been blasted into a million pieces the spell will be broken and the Hags free to return," Hansraj continued.

"But how?" Janki questioned.

"That is what Hansraj and I are going to continue working on," Joseph replied. "That's if Hansraj would be willing to assist me?"

Hansraj nodded. "Of course. I think I've seen enough evidence for me to believe that something untoward is happening. I don't know what it is. But the actions of my sons and events over the last few hours are leading me to believe that there is validity in your story."

Hansraj looked to his wife, who now couldn't say anything as her mud pack had tightened so much she was unable to move her mouth.

"Then preparations must be made," Faizal announced in an urgent tone. "We must find out where the agents have taken the stone and what their plans are!"

"And stop them!" Anuj added.

"Yes," Faizal agreed. "And stop them. But first you and Rajen need to spend time learning about the powers that have been given to you. You must be able to control them."

And with that the boys were led away by Mohammad to try and discover the extent of their new found gifts. They were led to the gym, which was right next to the pool. Hansraj and Joseph began pouring feverently over the books and manuscripts before them, trying to find more information.

Anita stood there whilst everyone dashed off in different directions. Faizal joined her, knowing that she must be incredibly concerned about all of this. She tried to speak, but the mud pack prevented her from doing so. Tired of the beauty treatment she chipped off the greenish mud.

"I am so sorry you have been drawn into this," he began. "I know this is not your fight, but we need your help."

Anita thought to herself for a moment and then looked him straight in the eye. "I can't deny what I've seen. What I want to know is if my children will ever be normal again, or will they always be a couple of super human 'freaks' who don't fit in! Do you have kids of your own?"

Faizal shook his head. "Alas, no."

"Then you have absolutely no idea whatsoever about how difficult it is to bring up two well balanced healthy children who are normal! Especially with the school system back home and peer pressure. Do you know how difficult that is?"

"No, I can assure you I do not!" Faizal admitted. "But your children are not 'normal' as you thought until only a short time ago."

"But they were until they ate that lollipop! A parent's job bringing kids up is difficult enough without them being able to race all over the place at the speed of sound and move things with their minds. How on earth am I going to be able deal with that?"

"We don't know if the juice has a life long effect, or whether the powers are with the boys for a limited period of time. When Joseph and your husband have investigated we will know much more."

Anita frowned. "You don't seem to know much about what's happening here, do you? I mean," she didn't give him time to answer. "You've had this 'Book Of Ted' for hundreds and hundreds of years. You've had all this time to really figure out what the guy was going on about and you didn't. You didn't even know that the stone, if I am going to buy into this story of yours, could be destroyed and then allow these 'Hag' things to come trundling back!"

"And where do my boys come into the equation? Surely there are enough of you to take care of these 'agents' on your own. You give my kids some juice which has now possibly made them even more uncontrollable than they were before, when if you'd looked after this stone properly in the first place, you wouldn't have needed us. I mean, fancy hiding it in an ice bucket for goodness sake."

Her voice was getting louder and louder. "You take yourselves so seriously, being this secret society and all that, and you let one little blue stone slip through your grasp as if it were wet putty! And why did it take my husband, a librarian from Leicester who doesn't know very much about you, or your history and all the problems you have now placed on our shoulders, to discover what your own librarian should have known long ago. After all, he doesn't seem to be doing much else other than studying these books!" The exasperation in her voice was more than evident and Faizal could see her point.

He was about to speak, not only his defence but also to defend the Guardians, but Anita simply held up her hand and took a couple of deep breaths.

"You know what?" she began. "You don't have to explain anything to me. All I wanted was a Christmas holiday in the sun, away from the usual stressful time at home. But no, nothing that simple could happen. Instead I find we are in the middle of some sort of fight for freedom! There's something to be said for staying at home and watching the endless television reruns!"

"I am sorry." Faizal apologised, not knowing what else to say.

Anita just looked at him and then smiled a small smile. "I'm a mother. I just want my kids to be OK! Is that too much to ask?"

Faizal took her by the hand. "Let's go and see what they're up to. I have no idea what their powers are or how we should use them. I don't know why the book said that Rajen would be the 'chosen one'. I don't know if the powers that have just been discovered will be with them for a few hours, days, weeks or they'll be with them forever. But there must have been something already within them that the juice simply activated. It seems to me, and I could be wrong, but whatever I'll say it anyway. They must have had these strengths all along and just didn't know about it!"

"And Hansraj?" Anita asked. "How come he can suddenly read ancient script which your guy, even after all the years he's been looking at it, couldn't understand!"

"There are strange powers at work here. Even though it is my destiny to help save Goa, I still don't know all the answers," he admitted.

"That's a big responsibility," Anita nodded. "I am not sure what I'd do if I were in your shoes. Probably be very scared."

Faizal smiled. "I'm not scared for me, just for Goa if we do not stop the Hags."

Anita could see that Faizal was very worried indeed. He was as confused as everyone else as to the path they must take to ensure that Goa remained free from the tyrannical Hags.

She decided not to be too hard on Faizal, and even though these were not the holiday plans they had arranged, things could be much worse. Anita still wasn't convinced about any of this. It was probably the sceptical side of her coming through as she was the realist in a family full of dreamers. Still she couldn't deny what she had seen and it defied logical explanation.

For now she would go along with everything, but the moment her family were threatened by anyone, or thing, they'd feel the full depth of her anger, of that everyone could be assured.

Let's Not Forget The Hags

Now the Hags were so convinced that their plan was going to work, that the agents would indeed come through, destroy the stone and provide them with the way to get back to Earth, that they had already started packing.

Hags lived for a very long time, as long as they have the precious turquoise to give them their life force, and their supply of turquoise was drastically depleted. Hags were both male and female in the same body. They were quite large, more pear shaped than anything else. They were covered with warts, had long hair, resulting in so many split ends you wouldn't believe, and kind of dull green coloured eyes which made them look rather sleepy.

They smelt very odd, a bit like a cross between a festering old sausage which has been left in a corner of the sofa under grandma's favourite cushion and a sweaty tennis shoe. As you can imagine, it wasn't very pleasant.

Anyway, as Hags lived for a very long time they only had baby Hags when they were in their last three years of life, which was usually about two hundred and fifty six years, give or take a year. Each Hag would only be able to have two baby Hags, though most only ever had one.

The Hags could have babies by themselves, as they had both male and female reproductive organs. This also happens in some plants, and life forms such as flatworms. A baby Hag could be created inside another Hag using the parents cells to create an exact replica.

All it would need was another Hag to place their hand on the "third eye," which we all have and is at the very centre of the forehead and is the first sign of rebirth.

For the Hags though, their first sign of their readiness for rebirth was the growth of a very large ugly wart on the end of their nose!

There were about four thousand Hags alive in Nowhere and they all wanted to return to Earth.

You see, Nowhere was bland. There was no landscape as such. No beaches. No oceans and no cities. There was just a big castle, where the Hags lived, and it was a very big castle indeed to be able to house four thousand of them, and a hotel. The hotel was where the souls and ghostly images of their human victims were kept.

The Hags spent their time sitting around, ordering each other around and thinking of terrible and hurtful things they could do to people. But as they never went anywhere they hadn't been able to do the things they had been planning for so long.

They didn't really have any purpose in life. They didn't add anything to the joy of living or empowering the well being of others. Shame to be like that isn't it?

Anyway, they had seen what was happening in Goa in their crystal ball. You see, they could see what was happening, but because they couldn't come within one million miles of the Earth, they were not able to get messages to their agents on Earth. Except for only once a year, during the window of opportunity, which as we know is for only sixty four seconds. A whole year's planning and plotting had to be given to their agents at this one time.

They knew that the agents planned to destroy the stone the following evening as it was the Hags who had passed on the information about the special rock in the grounds of the temple at Ponda. It was their imprisoned scientists and astronomers who had made the calculations about the stars being in the right place, the rock being of the right height and the reaction which would happen if the Sacred Freedom Stone and the rock should come into contact.

The agents had informed the Hags of their success in stealing the stone, through the Hags' crystal ball. You see, it acted rather like a silent television. The Hags could see what was happening, but were not able to hear. So when the agents had managed to get their grubby little hands on the stone they used sign language to tell the Hags that the plan was going to be put into action on a certain date. And that date was tomorrow at 11.45pm.

The Hags were very excited. It was the kind of excitement you get when you're about to go on a school trip. They were busy packing as much as they could. But their method of transportation was small to say the least so they wouldn't be able to take too much with them.

You see, they didn't have supersonic, light speed space ships which could travel at warp speed. They had… rickshaws.

Now, when the Hags were ruling Goa, rickshaws were small carts pulled by humans. As time went on these handpulled rickshaws changed to motorised ones. They had little engines in them that were only a bit more powerful than your everyday lawnmower. But that's the way that a lot of people dash from one place to another in Goa these days.

A few years ago, when the sixty four second window came about, the Hags chose to take fewer humans that year and steal as many of these motorised rickshaws as they could. You see, they had been planning their return for such a long time that they were trying to make sure that they'd thought of everything. And, of course, they needed transportation.

So they managed to steal six hundred and twenty eight motorised rickshaws from the city of Panjim and transport them to their castle in Nowhere.

There was a great deal of confusion in Panjim the following day. No on knew where the rickshaws had gone. And why would someone take so many of them. No one knew. The Guardians had their suspicions, though, but could not prove their theory until a couple of years later.

The Guardians had needed to get a spy into the Hags' castle in Nowhere for a very long time and no one had had any ideas of how they would be able to do this. It was Joseph who came up with a scheme and it worked.

They recruited a fish called Bill and trained him to the highest of agent training standards and then took him to their secret laboratory. There they placed Bill in a state of suspended animation, which means although he was still alive, he was in a very deep sleep. Then they waited for the sixty four second window to open.

Now, although the Guardians knew at exactly what time the window would open, they did not know the precise location of where the Hags would strike. Can you imagine if they had told all the people of Goa to watch out as on this particular night there were going to be these ugly things called Hags and they were going to steal your souls, whilst keeping your body here on Earth in a parallel dimension? They would have been locked away in the loony bin!

Although many knew about the Hags and the stories of

what went on years previous, they thought they were just "stories," old folk tales, legends if you like. They were to be taken with a pinch of salt and not given serious consideration.

Which is why the Guardians hid away and became a secret society as they knew people these days would not believe them.

Now, back to Bill. Because Bill was in a deep sleep, but his soul was as active as anyone who was walking around, he was highly likely to be taken by the Hags, without them even knowing. You see they'd be so busy taking humans, changing them into ghostly images and imprisoning their bodies in this parallel dimension, that they wouldn't notice a little fish with a walkie-talkie hidden amongst the souls being taken.

For two years they placed Bill in locations where there had been reports of missing persons. The first year the Hags did not take anyone from that place again. The second time they did and that's how Bill came to be in the Hags' castle in Nowhere.

He just slipped into the fish tank in the head Hags' study and after having a few run ins with the other fish in the tank, particularly the electric eel who was very spoilt and opinionated, he began his daily reports to the Guardians. The problem was he could only stay in the fish tank and from there see and hear only a little of what they were planning.

The Hags, on the other hand, were not able to place anyone in the Guardians' hide out. The Guardians had learnt about trust and keeping their group to as few people as possible, especially after the story of the telltale many years before, who had given away the details written in "The Book Of Ted." They had also discovered another means of keeping their activities a secret.

When Bill had told them about the Hags' crystal ball, Joseph went about finding a way to prevent them from being able to see into their hideout.

He researched and researched but could not find anything which would be able to "cloak" them from the prying eyes of their enemies. You see, the Hags didn't know where the exact location of the Guardians hideout was, but they soon would.

Joseph was walking along one of the many golden beaches in Goa, Colva Beach, where he spent a great deal of time as he liked walking, especially on sand with the sea gently lapping at his feet. Colva Beach was the longest unbroken stretch of white sand in the whole of Goa, almost twenty five kilometres, which meant Joseph could just walk and walk.

On one of these walks he stopped off at a beach shack for a drink of mango juice. As he was sitting relaxing and keeping out of the hot sun for a little while, he noticed a brightly coloured pot with a plant in it. He asked the lady who ran the shack, whose name was Elaine, what the plant was. She told him it was Tulsi, or Holy Basil, and that it protected her and her family.

Joseph asked what it was that she was being protected from. She told him that it was at her mother's insistence that they have brightly coloured pots of Tulsi everywhere they lived as the "ones from up high" would not be able to see them.

Joseph thought about this for a short while and then it clicked. He thanked Elaine and raced back to the big house, on the way buying many brightly coloured pots and small Tulsi plants.

Everyone at the house thought that he was being a little

strange at first when he began placing these pots everywhere. After placing all the plants he could around the house he explained himself.

Pulling out a map of Goa he showed where there had been reports of missing persons over the hundreds of years it had been since that Hags had been stealing people's souls. He overlaid this map with another which showed where Tulsi plants grew.

It then became clear to the Guardians what he was showing them. Wherever there were Tulsi plants, the Hags were not able to use their crystal ball to guide them. It acted like some sort of natural "cloaking" device, probably by giving off some sort of scent which altered the molecules surrounding it, twisting the paths of light and therefore preventing the Hags from being able to observe.

The Guardians already knew that the Hags' eyesight was extremely poor and this "twisting" of light made observation impossible. This was a most interesting discovery, that the scent of a natural organic plant could actually alter the light molecules surrounding it. A scientific breakthrough!

Many people in Goa had these plants outside their houses, but no one had ever really thought about the real reason why. Because it had been given the name Holy Basil, many assumed it was because of religious reasons and it would protect them. And, to a point, they were right. It was protecting them. It was protecting them from the Hags.

Superstitions, stories, myths, legends and history all mix together you see. It is more than likely that most of the stories and legends you read have elements of truth in them. Sometimes the fantastical parts of the story seems to take over and people only remember these, as they're often the best bits, but there are other parts of these stories which have actually happened!

So, the Hags were busy packing up their rickshaws, readying themselves for the return to Goa. Bill wasn't able to see much of what was going on, but with all the activity he knew something was up.

There was another reason why they were packing as much as they could. You see they had planted explosive devices throughout Nowhere. At exactly 11.45pm they would explode, completely destroying Nowhere, but the force the explosion created would be the energy they needed to push them right across space and back to Earth. A bit like a huge jet propulsion burst.

After all, they could not simply rely on the small rickshaw engines, they'd run out of petrol before they'd even covered the first few miles. The Hags were so sure that they were returning to Earth, that in order to do so they were prepared to destroy the whole of Nowhere to be able to make their wish come true.

The problem with this scheme was that if for some reason the agents did not succeed, Nowhere would explode, the energy created would force them forwards, but they would be then be pushed against the spell wall that Mikey had created to prevent the Hags from returning to Earth.

When the energy from the explosion met with the energy from the spell wall, which was generated by the millions of stars bouncing energy to and from each other, the result would be catastrophic for the Hags. They would be vapourised into nothingness.

In short, the entire Hag species would be wiped out in a bright flash of light!

From his hiding place, on the artificial bridge in the fish

tank, with the electric eel with an attitude problem, he was able to see a couple of the plans the Hags had drawn up.

Bill could see the outline of a temple and a rock, with another rock on top and a beam of bright light shooting upwards. It then looked as if the light was bouncing off things, but he couldn't make out what these were.

He stretched as far as his fish body would allow him to do so and saw that there was writing on the bottom. There was a time and a date written. He reached up and out of the tank as he still could not see.

There! There it was. He could see the time and date. Oh no! He pulled out the walkie talkie and radio to Faizal.

"Agent Bill here," he spoke as quickly as he could. "It's tomorrow night... 11.45... in a temple, on a big rock - some sort of stone on top, rock in grounds of temple behind plants, beam of light, they're packing, preparing to return. I can hear the engines of the rickshaws starting... it tomo..." The radio signal went dead.

On Earth Faizal twisted and turned the radio tuning button, trying to in vain to pick up Bill's signal again.

He raced to the library where Joseph and Hansraj were still pouring over the volumes of bound records.

"It's tomorrow," he exclaimed. "They are coming tomorrow..."

And with that he relayed the rest of Bill's message. Joseph and Hansraj renewed their efforts and rigorously searched for more information.

As Bill began to wake his vision was blurred. He could not see straight. Then things became much clearer. He was lying on the floor, under the table where the fish tank was situated. He tried to remember what had happened. He remembered talking to Faizal and then everything going blank.

He'd fallen! That's what had happened. Bill had fallen out of the fish tank and onto the floor.

He used his fins to prop himself up, rubbed his eyes and gasped when he saw danger approaching!

A cat. And it was coming straight for him. Oh no! Oh no! Then everything went black...

More Discoveries

Rajen and Anuj had been busy in the gym, working with Mohammad to discover exactly what powers the juice had given them. It became clear that Rajen had the "power of the mind."

If he concentrated hard on something, he could make it do what he wanted. It wasn't just the ability to move an object from one place to another. He could also make someone stop doing something, but only for a few seconds. He couldn't make people do what he wanted, although he could move them from one place to another, and he could freeze things in time, again only for a few seconds.

Anuj's powers were far more sporty. He could zoom from one place to another faster than the speed of light. All you could see was a bright flash and then feel a gust of wind as he moved around the room. Again, he could only do this in short burst as it took up a lot of energy.

Mohammad was, by profession, a school gym teacher. However, the school where he taught was for young adults who had special gifts. He had seen some fantastically amazing things in his time, but had never seen powers as intense as these. It was his opinion that in time, if the juice was found to have changed these boys' molecular make up forever, they would be able to harness their powers and increase their control of them to a much greater degree. There wasn't time for this right now and what Mohammad was trying to do was focus both Rajen and Anuj to concentrate on maintaining full control of their new-found abilities.

It was a little bit chaotic at first, with Rajen moving Anuj all over the place without asking and then Anuj retaliating by zooming everywhere, picking up Rajen without him even realising it and throwing him in the pool. There was a lot of shouting, flashing of bright lights and splashing, with the occasional whining sound of one of them shouting "stop it" to the other.

Mohammad more than had his hands full, but eventually calm and order was established and both boys started listening to their teacher and began following his advice.

Anita, who had now showered and washed off her mud pack, entered the gym and watched her sons. They were obviously highly delighted with what was happening. Anita was convinced, now more than ever, that these changes were here to stay and was trying to alter her mind set in order to deal with this. How on earth was she going to explain this to everyone back home? The mind boggled!

"Mum," Rajen shouted across to her. "Look!" And with that he lifted a plant pot and made it move from one side of the room to the other. He then lost his concentration and the plant pot fell to the floor and smashed.

"No," Mohammad stepped over. "Rajen, concentrate on lifting the pot, freezing it mid-air and then lowering it to the ground gently. You will break everything otherwise. You must learn control."

"Yes Mohammad," Rajen replied and then began working on other items around the room, lifting them up high in the air, making them cross the room and placing them down again gently. There were a couple more breakages, but after only a short time he was beginning to get the hang of it.

Anita could see that Anuj was having a whale of a time, racing around all over the place.

"Does he ever get tired?" she asked Mohammad.

"Thankfully, yes!" the instructor replied with the sound of relief in his voice. "Their powers only last for short bursts. It takes them a few minutes to recharge and then off they go again. But after three or four bursts, they need a while to recover."

"Thank goodness!" Anita replied under her breath. She could just imagine what a pain they were going to be at home in Loughborough!

"Gentlemen," Mohammad called out to the boys. "I think that's enough practice for now. Let's join the others in the library and see if there are any developments!"

Surprisingly there wasn't a word of complaint from either of them. They joined Joseph, Hansraj, Janki and Faizal in the library.

It was getting very late indeed. The time was now 3.45 in the morning. They couldn't stop though. Bill had told them that they had until 11.45 that night. Time was fast running out and so far no one had any answers.

Despite searching through the many books and maps, no one had managed to identify the exact temple Bill had spoken about in his last radio broadcast. Something about a stone, in the grounds of a temple. But there were so many temples and more than a few of them were surrounded by rocks of all kinds. Where were they going to begin?

Rajen and Anuj were given glasses of freshly squeezed mango juice as using their powers drain the body of both energy and liquid. They needed rehydrating, replacing the fluid they had lost.

They sat quietly at a small table to one side of the library, whilst the adults continued with their search for the particular temple Bill had told them about.

The Guardians had their agents scouring all the temples in Goa. No one had yet called in to confirm that they'd found a big rock in any of the temples' grounds.

Rajen remembered that his computer game was in his jacket pocket. He had been playing with it when they were in the TV room, but put it in his pocket when he and Anuj went swimming.

He turned it on and the screen burst into life. He was now on level eight. Rajen didn't know exactly how many levels there were to this game, as the packaging didn't tell him and the rule book stopped after level five...

A thought suddenly came to him. Level five was when the... hold on!

Level one was flying the plane, which he did...

Level two was deciding which vial of liquid to drink, either the one with sleeping potion or the one with the life giving force...

Level three was fending off an attack when the enemy tried to kidnap you...

Level four was where, if you had drunk the life giving juice, you would learn to harness your powers... and now...

Rajen was about to enter level five!

He clocked on the "play" button and then began. The game took him into a room, it looked like a library, there were books, maps and diagrams everywhere. There were flashes on the screen, flashes of an alien species who were climbing into some strange looking craft.

The crafts looked familiar to Rajen. For a moment he couldn't recall where he had previously seen them. Then it came to him. They were rickshaws, just like the ones they had here in Goa...

He stopped. He looked to Anuj, who was snoring, obviously tired after all his racing around and showing off his new powers. Rajen then looked at his parents and the others by the table.

He looked down at the game again and then back to the group in front of him. It was the same. It was exactly the same. They were in the same positions as the characters in the game. The game beeped loudly and a warning flashed.

It read: "You have two lives left. Two lives only. Use them wisely." The message then vanished and the image of the group at the table became clear again.

Raised voices at the table made Rajen look up again. The adults were obviously getting very frustrated.

He looked at the game again. The picture remained the same. What was happening? Was this a game or was it real?

Rajen pressed "continue" and the game started. It led him deep within the room. Then suddenly there were blasts of light from little holes in the wall. Rajen ducked his character behind a statue of someone who was obviously famous, otherwise they wouldn't have made a statue of him.

He looked at the name inscribed on the stone base. It read: "St. Francis Xavier." Rajen flipped the game over and looked at the front. There it was. The title of the game "The Life Force Of Xavier." Suddenly it all made sense to Rajen, as he remembered what Faizal had told him.

Legend has it Xavier was known with considerable affection as "Goencho Sahib," or the "Apostle of the Indes." Xavier travelled all over the place, trying to convert people such as Hindus, the Shinto Buddhists and other religions to the Catholic faith. He died of a fever in

1552 and after being buried in various places, he was eventually buried in Goa in 1554. Now every time they exhumed his body it remained intact, it was not decomposing, which is what is supposed to happen after you have died. There are reports that there was still warm blood flowing through his veins, even many years after he had died.

Everyone saw this as a miracle and in 1622, after many more tests had been carried out he was made a Saint.

Rajen flipped the game over again and continued to play.

He dodged the light rays as much as he could. But there were just too many of them. In the distance he could see a long box. It looked like a coffin, but rather than it being made of wood it was made of silver, and there were glass panels so you could see inside. Creepy!

Rajen had played so many of these games that he knew he had to get to the coffin. The next clue was hidden in it somewhere. It was his gut feeling, and when playing games like this one he had learned to go with his gut feeling as it had always seen him through.

He tried to move out from behind the statues, but was forced back into hiding by the sheer number of blasts. He was going to need some help. He saw the flashing indicator, telling him that he had two lives left. He knew he was going to have to use one of them right now.

Without hesitation he accessed the life and out of the wall burst a figure. Rajen couldn't make it out at first. The figure raced forwards towards the silver box, dodging all the light rays. Within seconds the figure had reached the silver coffin and pulled the huge wooden switch on the wall. In an instant the beams of light ceased and the room was quiet.

Slowly Rajen stood, looking at the walls to make sure the coast was clear. He looked at the figure by the silver coffin who beckoning him over.

Rajen slowly walked towards the figure and as he moved closer, stopped. His jaw dropped at what he saw. No way... It was Anuj, the figure in his computer game looked like Anuj. Rajen dropped the game suddenly, making everyone at the table turn.

"Are you alright son?" Hansraj asked.

"Yeah," Rajen nodded nervously. "I'm fine."

"You sure?" Anita pushed. "You look pale..."

"No, I'm fine. No problem," Rajen assured them with a smile. "I'm fine, just dropped the game." He reached down and picked it up. "Sorry, just being clumsy."

The adults turned back to looking at the books and continued with their search. Anita shot Rajen just one more inquisitive look and seeing that he was alright, joined the others.

Rajen quickly looked at the computer screen again.

"You're such a geek!" the character grinned. "Don't be a butterfingers and keep a hold of the game next time!"

Rajen gasped. It was Anuj. He looked up from the screen and turned to face his brother, who was still snoring away. Rajen sighed and stared at the computer screen. The character continued.

"You've used one of your lives to create me." he informed him. "You have one left and then you're on your own! What do you want to do?"

Rajen didn't press any of the buttons. Sweat was forming on his upper lip. He licked it away. Tasted very salty and of mango. Rajen looked at the table of adults who were obviously getting nowhere, and then back at the game. If the game was "reality," maybe this was the clue they needed! What if it wasn't though? He would waste his chance!

"The clock is ticking," the character urged him.

Rajen wiped his mouth and then decided. He pressed the button which would release the last one of his lives.

"Good choice, Rajen," the character grinned. Rajen was gobsmacked. It even knew his name. "Right then, listen and listen carefully 'cause I'm only going to say this once. You need to go to the Basilica Church, in Old Goa. There you will see a casket like this one, which has the remains of St. Francis Xavier in it. At the rear of the casket is a slot. Into this slot you must put the cartridge which you currently have in your computer. After you have done this you will not have the chance to retrieve the cartridge. Xavier will tell you what to do from there on. Good luck!"

The screen went blank. Rajen pressed the "play" button, but nothing happened. He then pressed every button on the machine. Still nothing happened. He was so angry and frustrated that he threw the game onto the floor where it smashed into many pieces.

Everyone looked around. No one spoke.

Anuj grunted and then awoke with a start, rubbing his eyes.

"What?" he blurted. "What's happened?"

"Rajen?" Faizal asked, curiosity filling his face.

"Son," Hansraj stepped towards Rajen. "What is is? Something has happened?"

Rajen looked to Anuj. Now Anuj never showed his feelings as it wasn't cool, but he could see that his baby brother was frightened. Anuj took Rajen's hand and pulled him close and gave the biggest hug. No, Anuj had forgotten that his strength had increased and, as he squeezed, he almost squeezed the living daylights out of Rajen, only stopping when his brother began to choke.

"Sorry!" he said, still holding on to Rajen.

"We have to go to the silver box, in the church," Rajen

began, stuttering a little.

"What?" Faizal moved closer.

"The church with the box, the old man," he wiped his snotty nose. "Xavier!"

"The remains of St. Francis Xavier?" Joseph called out, removing his glasses.

Rajen nodded, as he broke free from his brother's grip, reached down and picked up the cartridge which had come out of the game. He stood up and went back to Anuj who gripped his hand, assuring him that everything was alright.

"Why?" Joseph asked.

"We just do," Rajen looked him straight in the eye and with the most authoritative voice he could muster. "And we go now!"

They raced to the Basilica Church and to the casket housing the sacred remains of St. Francis Xavier...

Something Strange
On The Radar Screen

All was quiet at NASA, the space agency in America. Although there's always loads happening in space, like shooting stars, meteors, orbiting satellites and the like, there was nothing unusual appearing on the radar screens that day.

Tom Hamilton had been working at NASA for years. He had seen just about everything and anything to do with the exploration of space. That was until he saw the strangest looking blip on his screen.

He looked closer and tried to see what it was. The satellite image was coming from the other side of the galaxy beyond the one after the Milky Way. So it was a very long way off. This particular NASA satellite was very powerful and had a huge telescope on it which could project very clear pictures of what was going on out there.

Tom looked again and then picked up the red telephone beside him.

"Commander Deming, I think you'd better come and take a look at this!" He squinted his eyes, still trying to reassure himself of what he was seeing.

"What is it Tom?" asked his superior.

"Ma'am..." Tom couldn't believe what he was seeing or what he was about to say. "I'm picking up something a little strange on the screen, Ma'am!"

"Any idea what it is?"

"Well, Ma'am," Tom stammered. "If I'm not mistaken I think we're looking at fleet of ships positioned about one million miles from Earth."

"What?!"

"That's right, Ma'am, they're holding position and haven't advanced any further." Tom checked the data in front of him. "Yep, that's right, Ma'am, they're holding a position one million miles from Earth."

"I'm coming down there!" Commander Deming bellowed and slammed down the phone.

Moments later the door at the rear of the control room opened and Commander Deming and her Generals burst in. Other staff in the control room were gathering around Tom's radar screen. Their faces were filled with puzzled expressions.

"Make way here," Commander Deming called out, easing her way through the group. "Now let me see for myself!"

Commander Deming took a look at the screen, wiped her eyes and then took another look, just to make sure that she wasn't seeing things.

"What in blue blazes!"

"What do you make of it, Ma'am?" Tom asked.

Commander Deming took another long look and turned to her colleague.

"Tom, if I'm not mistaken," she gulped. "There's about six hundred and twenty eight Indian styled rickshaws one million miles from Earth..."

The Sun Rises Over Basilica Church

The sun was beginning to rise on the horizon as the car sped along the dusty roads towards Old Goa. This was once the capital of Goa, but after a plague hundreds of years ago, the elders moved to Panjim and established that city as the new capital.

There are many churches in Old Goa. When it had been a Portuguese colony they had built church upon church in honour of the Catholic faith.

The car sped through the metal gates and screeched to a halt in front of the main doors to the Basilica Church. There were other Guardians waiting for them, all eager to see Rajen and his family as word had already spread about the special powers they had been given.

In order that the Hags could not see them, they all were wearing a small piece of Tulsi in his/her top pocket. Anita, Hansraj, Anuj and Rajen had all been given their own before they left the house. At this critical stage, Faizal and the rest of the Guardians couldn't take any chances and let the Hags know of their exact location, even though the Hags knew that Rajen and his family were with the Guardians.

Faizal led them through the heavy wooden doorway and into the church. They walked towards the altar and then turned right just in front of it. There Faizal stopped. In front of them was the silver casket of St. Francis Xavier.

Rajen just stared at it. In the sides were glass windows so you see the actual body of Xavier.

Rajen was a little scared at first. I mean, this was a guy who had been dead for hundreds of years and he could see his body! Rajen slowly walked towards the silver casket. Anita stepped forwards to help her son. She took hold of his hand and they walked towards the casket together.

Rajen turned to his Mum and smiled. "It's OK Mum," he squeezed her hand tightly. "I'll go the rest of the way on my own."

"You sure?"

"Yep."

Anita stepped aside and Rajen continued. The others watched from a distance, not knowing what would happen, if anything, and not wanting to get in the way. Some of them, especially Mohammad, were actually a bit scared, but adults don't very often like saying that they're scared.

Rajen slowly climbed the wooden steps, as the casket was on a raised platform. He could see the body of Xavier very clearly now and he didn't feel even the remotest bit scared. He went right up close to the glass and looked in.

"Yep," he said quietly to himself. "He's dead alright!"

Rajen then looked around the sides of the silver box to see if there was a long thin slot into which he could slot the computer game cartridge he had just pulled out of his pocket. He ran his fingers over the highly detailed silverwork. It was very beautiful.

As he felt along the casket his finger reached a little lion's head. It was just there for decoration, but seemed, in Rajen's opinion, to be a little out of place.

He pressed it. Nothing happened. He pressed again and he felt a small rumble. Rajen didn't even flinch. He pressed the lion's head again, this time much harder. It went right in. For a few moments nothing happened and then a row of silver roses, which formed a decorative border, slid to one side to reveal a thin rectangular opening which was just big enough for the computer cartridge to fit in.

Rajen took a deep breath and pushed the cartridge into the opening. He turned to the others and gave them the "thumbs up" sign. They all sighed and waited to see what would happen next.

It took a few minutes and there was a lot of worry and tension filling the air but then suddenly the silver casket began filling with smoke. The smoke was contained inside the casket, none of it was escaping into the church itself.

Rajen stepped back and climbed down the steps backwards, not taking his eyes off the silver casket for a single second.

Suddenly, without warning, the top of the casket slid off, there was a bright flashing light and out burst St. Francis Xavier. Everyone just stood and watched, their eyes and mouths wide open, as he jumped out of the casket, stretched his arms above his head, let out the loudest yawn you've ever heard and then bounded down the steps two at a time and stuck out his hand to Rajen.

He wasn't decomposed like he looked when he was lying in the casket. He had brown hair, which was thinning a bit on top, brown eyes and milky white skin which had a bit of a sun tan and needed a wash. Simply amazing!

"Hi there Rajen," he beamed a big smile. "Francis Xavier, I believe you need to have a bit of a chat with me, well that's what Mikey said would happen if the Hags ever stole the Sacred Freedom Stone!"

Mohammad fainted.

Anuj nodded his head – "Cool!"

Rajen Talks With Xavier

Xavier placed his arm around Rajen's shoulder and they began to walk around the church. Xavier looked at the altars, decorations and shrines, a smile filled his face, as if seeing them brought back happy memories. Rajen noticed.

"You're smiling?"

"It's been a long time since I've had the chance to walk." He replied. For a moment he was silent, as though lost in thought, but quickly snapped out of it and turned to Rajen, crouching down to whisper in his ear while looking behind to make sure the others weren't close enough to hear.

"I don't have much time Rajen," he explained, rubbing his eyes. "Mikey's spell will only work for a few minutes and I want to help you. Now listen carefully. You need to go to a temple in the town of Ponda. The temple is called the Safa Masjid. It was one of the only temples to survive the excesses of the Inquisition. Now, the Hags' agents will be moving the stone there today. They will no doubt be performing their ritual this evening..."

"At 11.45!" Rajen interrupted.

Xavier nodded and placed his finger on Rajen's lips. "Right. Please. No more interruptions. Listen as this is important. There is an underground tunnel which links this temple to a ruined hilltop fort which is about two kilometres away by the coast. You will need to go to the fort, the exact location of which is on this piece of paper and also shown is the entrance to the tunnel," Xavier handed Rajen the paper.

"Thanks."

"Now the tunnel will open up in the temple grounds just behind the rock you are looking for. You and Anuj are the only ones who can save the day. You will have to wait until the agents have almost placed the Sacred Freedom Stone on the rock. You will see the stone beginning to glow. It is then that you must act. Before the stone has generated enough power to activate its beam of light and actually touch the other rock, Anuj must rush forwards and take it from the top of the rock. With his speed no one will be able to stop him.

"However," Xavier waved his finger at Rajen. "When you come out from the tunnel you will be seen by the agents, and as there will be hundreds, maybe thousands of them, you could well be overpowered. This is where you come in. You have the ability to 'freeze' people, but only for a few seconds. You must come out of the tunnel immediately after Anuj races for the stone, and 'freeze' everyone. This will take all the strength you have as there are so many of them. It's not going to be like anything you've experienced up until now where you have frozen only one person. It could take all your power and drain away your life force completely! Are you following this?"

Rajen nodded.

Xavier continued. "Anuj must then take the stone, and together you must travel across the country to the north of Goa, to a small fort, which has now been turned into a hotel. This is on top of a plateau. Inside the cobbled courtyard is the Chapel of Saint Anthony. If you have been successful there will be someone waiting for you there, someone you will need to listen to as he will be your guide!"

"What do you mean?" Rajen looked puzzled. "Am I going somewhere?"

Xavier smiled and then stood. "My dear Rajen, this is just the beginning. Both you and Anuj are indeed the 'chosen ones' and there is so very much more that you both have to do!"

"What do you mean?"

"You and Anuj have become a part of the 'Light Fantastic'. You will discover the wonders of this phenomenon as you go." Rajen was about to ask another question, but Xavier stopped him. "All will become clear in time. There is so much to learn in life, so many questions! You do not need to know all the answers yet. You must save the stone and return it to its rightful place. The cycle will continue and both you and Anuj will go forwards and discover what 'it' is all about. You will travel far and eventually go beyond the 'Light Fantastic'. That's when you will really make a difference! But for now, stop the Hags returning as they will stop the cycle. Get the stone and take it to the chapel. For it is then that some of the answers to the questions you now have filling your head will be given..."

Xavier looked at the sun outside. "You must not try and stop the agents before they start to place the stone on the rock. You see there must be energy created so the ground will cave in. Goa will be free from the Hags' agents once and for all." Xavier could see the confused look filling Rajen's face. He smiled.

"Don't worry. You must wait for exactly the right time and then act. You will know when that time is. Now, I must return to my place."

Xavier led Rajen back towards the others, smiled to himself and whispered in the boy's ear. "Shall we have a little fun?"

He squeezed Rajen's shoulders and then jumped towards the group, who all looked as though they'd seen a ghost.

Xavier beamed and did something he always wanted to do. Be a cheesy game show host.

"Hi here," he called out with that larger than life persona so many game show hosts exude. "Francis Xavier here, welcome to the show. Tonight we have a special guest... now what's his name? Ah, yes, here it is! Rajen, Rajen Parmar. Rajen has come to us all the way from England and he's been selected from our studio audience as one of the 'chosen ones'. Let's give him a big round of applause." Xavier began clapping excitedly. The others, completely caught up in the moment, also clapped.

"Great, wonderful crowd we have here this morning, so happy to be here. We'll be passing around some refreshments a little later on in the show, pork vindaloo, sorpatel and xacuti for those who love the Goan specialities and for those of you from further afield, how about fish and chips? How quaint! Right then, before I go and let you guys get on with the show as it's all up to you now..." Xavier stopped and raised his hands in the air. "Please, repeat after me 'It's all up to us now!'" The group shuffled uncomfortably, not really knowing what was going on here. "Oh, come on guys, this little chap is going to need all the support you can give, let's see a little more effort here. And let's try that one again."

The group repeated Xavier. "It's all up to us now!"

"And again." Xavier encouraged.

"It's all up to us now!"

"Fantastic," Xavier beamed as he began to walk up the steps which led to the silver casket. "Absolutely fantastic, you all deserve a medal, if not a medal then a free mobile phone! How 'bout it?"

For some inexplicable reason the group all cheered. Xavier smiled and waved to them and then, in a flash of smoke, returned to the silver casket.

As the smoke settled the remains of St. Francis Xavier returned to their original state. Rajen looked at the casket and then to the piece of paper he had been handed by this extraordinary man. He opened it and looked at the ancient writing, writing he had never seen before.

Strange. He could understand every word and mark, even though he had never seen this language before. He looked up at the casket and then to the group. All were staring at him.

Rajen glanced at the paper again and as he did so the paper went blank and another message appeared.

Go forward, young Rajen, don't be scared. Go towards The Light Fantastic.

And then the words vanished as quickly as they had appeared. Rajen saw the original writing and symbols reappear. He looked towards the casket once again and Xavier was staring at him. The Saint winked and gave him the "thumbs up" sign. Rajen smiled and then Xavier turned his head and returned to his deep, deep sleep.

He could rest now. His job done.

Rajen turned to the others. "There isn't much time and I know what we have to do!"

Confrontation

The plan was quickly relayed to the group and they travelled towards the ruined fort Xavier had told them about.

There was a great deal of activity in Goa. There seemed to be so many people lining the roads, all of them heading towards the temple at Safa Masjid. The people looked directly forwards with no expression. It was very spooky.

The car sped towards the ruined fort, which, other than the Guardians who had already arrived, stood empty. It was in such a state of disrepair that many people had probably forgotten that it even existed.

After about an hour and twenty four minutes of searching, Janki had located the entrance to the tunnel Xavier had told them about. From here on in it was just Rajen and Anuj. A group of the Guardians had been placing Tulsi plants around the fort, so the Hags could not see what they were doing, whilst another group raced north to the Chapel of St. Anthony.

Anita and Hansraj stayed with their sons for as long as possible. Both the boys had been given flashlights so they could see where they were going as it was going to be so dark down there.

As the two of them stepped into the tunnel, Anita gave each of them a huge hug and wiped away a nervous tear.

"You both take care, look after each other!"

"We will Mum," Rajen assured her.

"See you later Dad!" Anuj waved as he stepped into the darkness and turned on the flashlight.

"You'd better!" Hansraj replied.

"Love you!" Anita called after them both as Rajen also stepped into the tunnel. Before he vanished into the darkness, he turned to face his Mum and Dad. "Don't worry, it'll all be OK. I am the 'chosen one'!"

"Me too!" Anuj corrected him.

Anita sighed and then turned to her husband. "The therapy bills are going to be huge when we get home!"

"We can always take out a second mortgage?" Hansraj suggested.

The boys moved onwards as quickly as they could. Even though the tunnel was very old and no one had been down there for hundreds of years, it was remarkably clear. Through the tunnel walls there were some roots of trees which had grown in the earth above, and in parts it was very damp and wet. These must be places where there was a well or a river nearby.

Everything was going alright until Anuj stopped. Rajen, not really looking where he was going, bumped into him.

"What's the matter?" he asked. "Keep going!"

"I would if we could!"

Anuj pointed his flashlight up ahead and Rajen could see the pile of earth completely filling the tunnel.

"What are we going to do?" Rajen asked.

Anuj thought for a moment and then had an idea. "Here," he handed his flashlight to Rajen. "Point this on the pile of dirt and grab my waist."

"What?"

"Just do as I say," Anuj instructed, taking hold of Rajen's other hand. "Now hold on."

Before Rajen knew what was happening, Anuj had raced forwards and was furiously beginning to dig. He started getting faster and faster. Rajen then realised what he was doing. He was using his powers to speed things up. As Anuj dug, the earth flew over Rajen's head and piled up behind them. They were burrowing their way through the blockage.

Rajen held on to his brother for all he was worth, whilst still trying to keep the flashlight pointed in the direction they were going.

There was a lot of earth. It must have been a very big cave in at some point, but eventually they broke through and the tunnel was clear again.

Anuj collapsed. Rajen crouched by his side.

"Anuj?" there was obvious concern in his voice

"I'll be fine, just give me a minute."

The boys sat there for a while until Anuj recovered from his energetic outburst and then continued onwards.

Although they were underground, there were parts of the tunnel which had broken through and they could see the sky above them getting darker. They knew that night was falling. It must have been around seven o' clock, as that's when the sun was due to set.

They continued onwards, dodging the protruding roots and digging through the much smaller piles of earth where the tunnel had collapsed over the years.

It wasn't long before they reached a set of stone steps, leading upwards in a spiral manner.

"This must be where the tunnel opens up into the temple grounds," Anuj told Rajen. "Do you have the map?"

"Yep."

"When we come out, where's the rock we need to find?"

Rajen held his flashlight over the paper and pointed it out to Anuj. "It's not too far, but they'll be loads of people around it. We are going to have to move fast."

"Too right we are," Anuj agreed.

They climbed the steps and upon reaching the top pushed open the rotten wooden door. As they looked out from their hiding place they could clearly see the masses of people surrounding the huge rock.

The rock was to one side of the grounds and there had obviously been lots of plants and shrubs covering it. These had been cleared away to create the large open area.

Rajen noticed that the agents had put up a big banner across the large building on the far side of the clearing. It read: "Welcome Home Hags."

Now they had to wait.

As the moon rose higher in the night sky the time had come. There was an unnatural silence as from out of one of the buildings stepped a group of cloaked people. There were six of them in total and between them they carried a box. The boys could just make out that the box was glowing. The Sacred Freedom Stone was inside!

As the group passed by, the others surrounding the rock opened up a small pathway and then fell to their knees.

The box was placed before the rock and opened. The blue glow was very strong. It seemed to get stronger as they brought it closer to the rock. One of the six took the stone out of the box and then thrust it high into the air. It was almost as if he were showing it to the Hags, who despite being a million miles away, could see what was happening through their crystal ball.

The Hags turned on their rickshaw engines. The time

was nearly right. They would rule Goa once again. Oh, what a wonderful thought that was to them all.

As the clock struck 11.45 the Hags' agent began to lower the Sacred Freedom Stone onto the rock. He struggled a little for as the two were brought closer together the power was beginning to surge through them.

"Ready?" Rajen asked Anuj, who was quickly tying up his laces even tighter.

"As I'll ever be."

As the clock chimed the final chime, Rajen and Anuj burst out from their hiding place.

"Go Anuj," Rajen shouted.

All heads turned. There was confusion. The Hags' agent, holding the Sacred Freedom Stone, looked up to see what was happening.

Anuj raced forwards, but there were just too many people getting in the way. He shouted to his brother.

"Rajen, just do it!"

Rajen concentrated as hard as he could. He could feel his energy being drained, but it didn't stop him. He focused even harder and remembered what the consequences would be if they did not succeed.

As he strained his concentration even harder it began to work. Everyone started to freeze. As they did so, Anuj leapt across their shoulders and towards the agent with the stone.

The agent looked at the others who were all about to move forward and help him, but were stopped when Rajen's powers reached them and froze each and everyone like statues.

The agent with the stone could see that Anuj was heading directly for him. It didn't take a rocket scientist to figure out that the boy was after the stone. The agent used all his strength to try and push the stone and rock together.

A million miles away the Hags could see what was happening through their crystal ball. They could see their return plans being thwarted and they were none too happy!

Anita, Hansraj, Faizal and the others were waiting at the Chapel, their fingers crossed. They could see the glow of light from right across the country. They knew the time had come. The fate of Goa was now in the speed and strength of the two boys.

Anuj was nearly there, though he could feel some of the people starting to move beneath him. He shouted back to Rajen.

"Are you OK?"

"I can't keep them frozen for much longer Anuj. Can't you hurry up?"

"I am going as fast as I can, just keep them frozen for a few more seconds."

The agent had almost made the stone and rock touch. If he succeeded then the Hags would return and things would be really bad. The rock and the stone were only millimetres away from each other. One more push from the agent in the cloak and it would all be over.

But just before the corner of the stone almost touched the rock, Anuj reached out and took hold of the Sacred Freedom Stone. The agent wouldn't let go though. Anuj tugged and pulled, but the agent just wasn't having any of it and held on for dear life.

Anuj knew that drastic measures had to be taken and he reached down and bit the agent's hand.

You have never seen someone jump so high or yelp so loud at the same time. Anuj grabbed the stone and raced back to Rajen, who was now on his knees as the energy he was giving out to keep the people frozen was draining his very life force.

As Anuj reached him, Rajen collapsed. The power had been too much, there was nothing left for him to give.

Anuj held Rajen in his arms, calling out his name again and again.

"Wake up! Wake up!"

But nothing. Rajen was as still as still could be.

Anuj looked up and saw people rushing towards him. He couldn't stay. He had to get the stone out of there. He picked up Rajen and with super human force and speed, raced right through the crowds, anger and frustration making him even more determined to get out of there.

As Anuj burst through the crowds and raced northward towards the Chapel of St. Anthony, the ground surrounding the rock began to rumble and open up.

"What's happening?" the crowd called out.

No one knew.

You see Goa is a mining country, particularly for iron ore, which is then shipped around the world to make cars and steel girders for buildings. The power created by the Sacred Freedom Stone and rock had shaken the ground so much that it had begun to break up and cave in. There were miles upon miles of mining tunnels under this part of the country and the ground was falling into the massive caverns below.

There was this loud cry from somewhere out in space, as the Hags knew their plan had been thwarted.

Then another explosion. They turned to see Nowhere disintegrate before their very eyes. They braced themselves for what was about to happen. Seconds later a huge energy wave engulfed them, pushing them towards Mikey's spell wall.

As the two energy forces met, with the Hags and their rickshaws caught in the middle, there was a blinding light and in an instant, quicker than it takes to bite the head off a jelly baby sweet, the entire race of Hags, some four thousand of them, were wiped out without a trace.

Just before the last of the Hags was vapourised, it sighed and rolled its eyes in despair.

"Trust humans to mess things up!"

Then silence. The star dust settled and the world was now finally free from the Hags and their horrible ways.

Anuj raced across Goa, faster than he ever imagined he could travel. All anyone could see was a blinding light flashing before them, followed shortly afterwards by a gust of wind.

He needed to get to the chapel as fast as he could. Within seconds he had arrived. He placed Rajen on the marble table. He was lifeless. Was this the end? Anuj couldn't bear it...

Mikey

Anita and Hansraj were beside themselves. Their son was lying lifeless in front of them and there was nothing that anyone could do.

Anita turned to Faizal. "Please help, there must be something you can do? Joseph, the books, where is the bit that will bring my boy back to life?"

Alas, no one had the answers Anita was looking for and so rightly deserved. Her son had come without choice, helped without hesitation, and now his lifeless body was laid out before them all.

Anuj was speechless. He stood alone to one side. He didn't want anyone to come anywhere near him. This wasn't meant to happen. Not Rajen! Not little Rajen!

His eyes welled with tears but he forced them back before anyone could see. He must be strong now.

Faizal joined Anuj. "I need you to give me the Sacred Freedom Stone. We must place it in the shrine."

Anuj snapped. "My brother is lying there and all you can think about is this stupid stone," he shouted, pulling the stone from his pocket. "Here, take it!" He thrust it into Faizal's hand and turned away.

Faizal felt terrible. He knew he must have seemed very heartless and cold, but he needed to place the stone in the small shrine at the side of the chapel. He was simply following the instructions left to him by Mikey.

Faizal slowly walked to the small shrine, which was hidden behind a gargoyle, and placed the stone in the slot. The stone was immediately pulled downwards and vanished from view. Faizal stepped back. The other Guardians gathered around Anita and Hansraj who would not leave Rajen.

The chapel did not have electric lights, the interior was illuminated by wooden torches of fire placed in metal brackets along the walls

There was a slight breeze. Suddenly it became a gust and the torches blew out. Darkness. Then from the shrine where Faizal had placed the stone a bright light burst skywards. It was so bright that they all covered their eyes for fear of being blinded.

The roof of the chapel ripped off and the wind became very strong indeed, gusting around, knocking over the chairs, tables and bookcases in the chapel. The group clung onto each other for all their worth. Anuj was the only one left alone. He grabbed hold of one of the statues and held on for dear life.

The gusts of wind were so strong that each of them was being lifted off the floor. Hansraj and Anita held on to each other, and to Rajen, who was as cold as stone and lying prone on the marble table.

Anuj looked upwards to see where the beam of light was going. Maybe they hadn't succeeded. Maybe they hadn't read the instructions properly and the Hags were going to come back after all. Maybe this had all been a terrible mistake and they shouldn't have taken the stone in the first place. It had briefly crossed his mind that maybe the Guardians were the ones who were bad and the Hags were good. Maybe they'd been lied to! But then again maybe not, as the evidence was too strong for him to really believe otherwise.

He just wanted his brother back. That's all.

The beam of light hit the nearest star, which then started bouncing it around from one star to another until the final star shot the beam of light straight back to the chapel and into the body of Rajen which was still lying on the marble table.

The gusts of wind became stronger and stronger and Anita lost her grip of her son.

"Noooo!" she cried out, but could not be heard above the phenomenal noise that was being created.

Then it stopped. In a heartbeat. The wind stopped. The noise stopped. It stopped so suddenly that they all fell to the floor. Silence. Total and utter silence.

All eyes looked to the beam of light shining from the stars into the lifeless body of Rajen. It was shining straight into his heart. Anuj ran forwards.

"Stop it," tears were falling from his eyes. "Leave him alone!"

Hansraj grabbed Anuj and held him tightly. No matter how hard Anuj tried to break free from his father's grasp, he could not, not even with his new super human powers!

They all watched silently as the light began to turn blue and then out from Rajen's body an image of a man rose.

The image rose high above the table where Rajen lay, floated across the room and set down in front of them on the ground. The light dimmed and there standing before them was the very man who had been guiding them all along. It was the ghostly image of Mikey!

The beam of light moved from Mikey back to Rajen, where it remained.

"Hi there," Mikey smiled. Before any of them could

reply he walked over to Rajen and placed his hand on the boy's brow. From his pocket he pulled a small glass container and from within it he produced the blue Sacred Freedom Stone. No one asked how he'd ended up with it.

Without hesitating for a second he took the stone in the palm of his hand and squeezed it gently. After a few moments the stone began to glow a reddish colour and then, from the bottom right hand corner, a small drop of juice appeared.

Mikey positioned the stone over Rajen's mouth and let the droplet of juice fall onto his lips. The stone produced a second drop and Mikey did the same thing again.

Nothing happened. Everyone moved closer. Mikey turned to them and held up his hand.

"Please don't come too close and crowd him. Let the boy breathe."

They waited. Then, in an instant, Rajen sat bolt upright and stared right at Mikey.

"You could have told them that the juice would've saved me!"

Mikey shrugged. "What can I say? I like drama!"

Anita and Hansraj raced forwards and hugged their son. Words eluded them all right now.

Rajen climbed off the table and began walking slowly towards Anuj. He picked up speed and rushed to his brother. They embraced.

"I thought you were gone!" Anuj whispered.

"Not for a long time. We have so much to do!"

Anuj was confused at first. Rajen led him to Mikey who was still holding the stone. Rajen faced Anuj.

"I need for you to drink two drops of the juice!"

Anuj didn't question. He just did. As with Rajen, the stone produced two drops of juice which fell on Anuj's lips. He licked them and the juice entered his system.

Mikey replaced the stone in the secret shrine and ushered everyone into the courtyard outside. He pointed upwards to the night sky, which was as clear as clear can be.

There were misty images flitting across the sky towards a bright light in the distance. The images were of people. They looked happy, almost relieved. Mikey turned to the group.

"These are the kidnapped human rejoining their souls from Nowhere. They are going home." He then pointed to the shoreline below them. There was a sharp cracking sound and then a burst of light. The parallel dimension had opened.

From the shores hundreds and thousands of people broke through and raced to join the images in the sky. Mikey continued. "These are the trapped bodies of the souls the Hags took. They need to be joined together before they can enter their new home, The Light Fantastic."

"At last they are free," he sighed.

Rajen held on to Mikey's hand. "What about you? You were kidnapped. Is your body going to join with you? Are you leaving us?"

Mikey smiled. "You, Anuj and I are just beginning young Rajen! There is no time to join with my body. When our work is finally complete, then I too can go home."

"What do you mean?" Anita asked. "What's this 'unfinished' work. I have lost my son once and by a miracle he has come back. I can't go through that again... neither of us can." She took hold of Hansraj's hand and pulled him close to her.

Mikey lowered his head. "It was decided many, many years ago that a certain boy, and his brother, would be the 'chosen ones'. They would help lost souls home, back to where they could finally rest after they had completed their tasks... their journey's end if you like."

"But why our boys?" Hansraj asked.

Mikey shrugged. "I cannot answer you that. They may be able to discover the reasons as they go through the different levels and tasks."

"But they will never be normal again!" Anita exclaimed.

"No, they won't. Which is unfortunate for you, but will help to save humankind."

"But haven't they done enough?" Hansraj was trying to take in all of this information.

"They have simply been 'tested'. The Hags indeed posed a great threat to Goa. But in time, we would have been able to banish them forever. There are other tasks which need their immediate assistance."

"They are coming home with us, aren't they?" Anita asked.

Mikey smiled. "They will continue with their lives as usual and be called upon when a task, or mission, demands. They are your sons, but we will need their help!"

Anita sighed. Mikey took hold of her hand. He reached out for Hansraj to give him his hand. He did. Mikey squeezed them gently.

"I know that all of this must be completely confusing and throwing you off balance. The boys will be looked after, I will guide them. That, as they say, is my department."

He gave their hands one last squeeze and then joined Faizal, Janki and Mohammad.

"Your job is complete. The Guardians, as a group to look after Goa and protect it from the Hags is no longer needed. But," and he pointed to Rajen and Anuj. "They are going to need a team to help them. Are you up to the challenge?"

The three of them didn't even have to give their answer a second thought, and nodded without hesitation.

Mikey joined the two boys at the side of the courtyard. They were watching the bodies and souls joining together in the sky and then racing as fast as they could towards the bright light in the distance.

"Where is The Light Fantastic?" Anuj asked.

"I have never been, as my job is not yet finished. I have the two of you to look after now. But, I'm told, it's a place of rest, of peace. It is a place where the individual mind, be it of any animal, fish, plant... anything, can find peace. It must be protected from forces which see it as a threat. This is why we must travel to places beyond The Light Fantastic and make sure it is not at risk from anyone, or thing, and is safe, forever!"

"But won't we have to die to go there?" Anuj frowned.

"Not in your case. You see you two are the 'chosen ones'. In time you will come to realise your full powers and eventual reason for being. Until that time, until your job is done, you have to protect others."

"That's a lot of responsibility!" Rajen noted. "Are we up to it?"

Mikey nodded. "I think you are." "And," he continued, pointing to the Guardians, "They'll help, and I will guide you."

"But where do we start?" Rajen persisted.

Mikey pointed to the beach. "By having a holiday, parasailing, swimming with dolphins, eating great food and being happy. We will meet again, when the time is right. But for now you both need to be boys. You need to live your life, you can't always help everyone! You just need to... live!"

Suddenly there was a blinding flash and into the room burst a cat holding a fish in its mouth. The fish was calling out.

"Help, it's me, Agent Bill. Get me out of this cat's mouth. He's going to eat me!"

Quicker than quick Rajen "froze" the cat and Anuj zoomed forwards, picked Bill out of the cat's mouth and placed him in the font near the altar.

As Rajen stopped his spell, the cat started to rise into the air and drifted out to sea. There it joined its body, which had been trapped in the parallel dimension and, without even looking back, it too began to race towards the light.

"I must go now," Mikey said and began to walk back towards the beam of light. "Before I do I have a little something for you." He handed Rajen a computer game cartridge. "From Xavier, you left it in his casket," Mikey whispered in his ear. "There might be something you want to have a look at!"

And with that Mikey stepped into the light, winked at the boys, waved to Anita and Hansraj and then vanished as the beam of light flickered out.

Rajen held the cartridge in his hand.

"Mum, I need to find a computer..."

Anita placed her finger on his lips and pulled both her sons together.

"I think that Mikey said you need to go and have a holiday and live, live, live!"

"And what does Mum say?" Hansraj joined them.

Anita thought for a moment. "Mum says... we all need ice cream... and then parasailing..."

"And jet skiing..." Anuj added.

"And scuba diving!" Rajen continued.

"And sleep!" Hansraj yawned.

"Oh Dad, come on!" Anuj gave him a playful punch in the shoulder. "We're on holiday. Time to have some fun... and to live!"

They left the chapel...

The adventure has begun...

Mr Dark

Written by Simon James Collier
Cover illustration by Gillian Martin

On a dark and misty evening last Autumn, Albert Evans, the
Prime Minister of England, gave a speech on national television
about how horrible and nasty the dark was, and how everyone should
band together to try and get rid of it. After his speech the
whole country was thrown into panic.

Never in the history of the world, had the dark been so
universally feared and disliked as it was now!

As the Prime Minister gave his speech, on the other side
of the galaxy, an evil, bitter and twisted creature clucked and
chuckled as he heard the minister's damning words.
*"Soon the galaxy will be mine - and there's nothing that
anyone can do to stop me!"*

The creature laughed out loud and all around him trembled.
They knew that he was the nastiest thing ever to walk the galaxy.

He was: the Pink Chicken with the dark sunglasses!

ISBN: 1-874342-10-5

The Return Of
The Pink Chicken

Written by Simon James Collier
Cover illustration by Gillian Martin

As peace returns to Earth after the defeat of the Pink Chicken, it seems that nothing will disturb the planet ever again. However, fate soon deals an unkind blow when out of a black hole in a distant galaxy the Pink Chicken finds himself cast back to the heart of the very city he was happy to be a million miles away from – London.

Dismayed by his previous bad luck, the evil piece of poultry decides to turn his unfortunate circumstances to his advantage by waging full-scale revenge on the planet he hates so much.

But the Pink Chicken's plans do not take into account the Earth's ever-faithful guardian, Mr Dark. Along with his intergalactic friends, Sydney and Captain Stardust, the battle to save the World from doom and gloom is joined by a new set of heroes, including the White Wizard of Carnaby Street, a million flying television sets, an Empress in disguise, a trifle with a *vision*, a bumper volume of bad TV jokes and a new young hero – *OMAR!*

ISBN: 1-874342-15-6

The Final Sponge Cake

Written by Simon James Collier
Cover illustration by Gillian Martin

It seemed as though the Earth was at last safe against the clutches of the evil Pink Chicken. But fate was yet again unkind and from the small planet he had been exiled to, he plotted and planned his revenge on Earth. As soon as Keith, the Pink Chicken's driver, had repaired the bright pink convertible that had so ignominiously blasted them into space and as soon as the Pink Chicken had eaten one last egg custard tart, they flew unnoticed back to our peaceful planet.

It was then that the *real* trouble began.

Meanwhile, the Queen of England had become something of an artiste, and was holding a huge exhibition of her latest sculptures at Buckingham Palace.

Everyone who was anyone was invited and the occasion promised to be one that everybody would remember and talk about for years to come. How right they were to think this - but with the entire kitchen staff kidnapped, the guards unaware and a whole host of smelly sewer rats eating away at the foundations, it was going to be an evening they would remember - but not for the reasons they all imagined.

Only Mr Dark, Richard, Omar and their friends can save the day and finish off the Pink Chicken once and for all!

Spooky Noises

Written by Simon James Collier
Illustrations by Louise Comfort

A young girl's imagination runs wild in the warmly reassuring
story, that things that go bump in the night are not always Green
Goblins from Ganooch, Fire-breathing dragons from Puffsville,
Ghosts from Ghostberry Farm, or even Trolls from
Trottersfield Snipe! But what can it be?

ISBN: 1-874342-05-9

George The Germ

Written by Simon James Collier and Michael Cooney
Illustrations by David Cockburn

Meet George the Germ, the family Grot, a host of flies and
the stunning "Queen of Clean", Belinda Beetle, in this
humourous collection of rhyming adventures.
Goop-stretching George squelches his way through school, holiday
resorts and a family picnic, before he finally meets the beautiful
Belinda, who makes him change his naughty ways.

With a message of health and hygiene, "George the Germ"
is ideal for both reading aloud to younger children and children
up to the age of 12 to read alone.

ISBN: 1-874342-00-8

Simon James Collier

Simon was born in Nottingham in 1967 and, upon graduating from the DeMontfort University in Leicester, went to work in Hollywood, California. Since returning to England, Simon has written and published ten books, staged eleven theatre productions, both in London and around the country, three of which he co-wrote, been a Picture Editor for over 400 magazines, books and/or periodicals, the Executive Producer of the 2001 London Cast Recording of "Elegies", and is an entertainment reviewer for BBC radio. He is currently a Trustee of The Globe Centre in East London, working with people affected by HIV and AIDS, and also the Chairman of BILAN which promotes health and social care of people from the "Horn of Africa" living in London.